Stranger in the Night

Hawk wasn't sure how much time had passed before he opened his eyes. He'd heard something. The lamp was lit and warm . . . sweet breath pushed against his face. He jerked his head back, snapped a hand toward his gun belt coiled over a bedpost, clawed the Russian from the holster, and clicked the hammer back.

A woman laughed and leapt back from the bed. "Easy, lover! It's me, Saradee Jones."

When Hawk's eyes focused, he saw her heart-shaped face framed by billowing, copper-colored hair. Her heart-stopping, high-breasted, round-hipped body, clad in only a dusty trail hat and a flimsy chemise . . .

"You must've been riding hard, last few days. Didn't think I could sneak into your room, much less light a lamp while you snored like a drunken sailor." She leaned down and kissed his cheek. "You're getting careless, Mr. Hawk."

Hawk aimed the cocked Russian at her. "How in the hell did you get in here? I told you next time I saw you, I'd kill you."

Chuckling, she leaned forward, her left hand nudging his pistol up into the deep crease between her breasts. She ran her fingertips along the gun's barrel, then down along his hand and wrist, tickling him with her nails. "Why don't you fire?"

ROGUE LAWMAN

BULLETS OVER BEDLAM

Peter Brandvold

BERKLEY BOOKS, NEW YORK

THE BERKLEY PUBLISHING GROUP
Published by the Penguin Group
Penguin Group (USA) Inc.
375 Hudson Street, New York, New York 10014, USA
Penguin Group (Canada), 90 Eglinton Avenue East, Suite 700, Toronto, Ontario M4P 2Y3, Canada
(a division of Pearson Penguin Canada Inc.)
Penguin Books Ltd., 80 Strand, London WC2R 0RL, England
Penguin Group Ireland. 25 St. Stephen's Green, Dublin 2, Ireland (a division of Penguin Books Ltd.)
Penguin Group (Australia), 250 Camberwell Road, Camberwell, Victoria 3124, Australia
(a division of Pearson Australia Group Pty. Ltd.)
Penguin Books India Pvt. Ltd., 11 Community Centre, Panchsheel Park, New Delhi—110 017, India
Penguin Group (NZ), 67 Apollo Drive, Rosedale, North Shore 0632, New Zealand
(a division of Pearson New Zealand Ltd.)
Penguin Books (South Africa) (Pty.) Ltd., 24 Sturdee Avenue, Rosebank, Johannesburg 2196,
South Africa

Penguin Books Ltd., Registered Offices: 80 Strand, London WC2R 0RL, England

This is a work of fiction. Names, characters, places, and incidents either are the product of the author's
imagination or are used fictitiously, and any resemblance to actual persons, living or dead, business
establishments, events, or locales is entirely coincidental. The publisher does not have any control over
and does not assume any responsibility for author or third-party websites or their content.

ROGUE LAWMAN: BULLETS OVER BEDLAM

A Berkley Book / published by arrangement with the author

PRINTING HISTORY
Berkley edition / April 2008

Copyright © 2008 by Peter Brandvold.
Cover illustration by Bruce Emmett.
Cover design by Steven Ferlauto.
Interior text design by Kristin del Rosario.

ISBN: 978-0-425-22066-5

BERKLEY®
Berkley Books are published by The Berkley Publishing Group,
a division of Penguin Group (USA) Inc.,
375 Hudson Street, New York, New York 10014.
BERKLEY is a registered trademark of Penguin Group (USA) Inc.
The "B" design is a trademark belonging to Penguin Group (USA) Inc.

PRINTED IN THE UNITED STATES OF AMERICA

10 9 8 7 6 5 4 3 2 1

For the Hi-Line couple:
John Anderson and Pam Burke,
remembering the horseback rides,
airplane rides,
Sadie and Shep,
and Friday nights with pistols and beer

1.

SOGGY STALKING TRAIL

FROM a night sky black as a tar pit, lightning slashed through the rain and knifed into a sprawling cotton-wood. Showering sparks sizzled as the storm loosed its wrath upon the world.

Thunder rumbled like cannon fire, shaking the earth.

The gods were angry. That's how it seemed to Gideon Hawk, riding his grulla mustang through a narrow draw, water up to the horse's hocks and sluicing off Hawk's broad-brimmed hat. The sky was dark as a blacksmith's apron, the air silver with the nickel-sized raindrops that had been pummeling him for the past two hours.

Thunder rumbled over the mountains enclosing him on three sides. Like fireworks, lightning lit up the stark, rocky, saguaro-studded terrain nearby.

It had been a long trail—three days' worth of hard tracking six killers and bank robbers from Cartridge Springs. When they'd hit the Stockman's Bank and the Wells Fargo office, the gang led by Shadow Nielsen and Skylar Parks had left town whooping like jackals and trig-gering lead, taking the banker's daughter hostage and leaving a young woman and her little boy sprawled across the boardwalk before the millinery shop, dead.

Hawk hadn't been in town that day. But news had spread over the telegraph wires.

When he'd heard that the sheriff's posse who'd followed the gang to the Territorial border had lost the trail in the badlands, Hawk rode to Cartridge Springs and quietly, anonymously took up the hunt.

Bona fide lawmen couldn't bring jackals like these to justice. It took a lawman unshackled by civilization's laws and society's rules—who enforced the law of the primitive—to give uncivilized lobos as these, who'd kill an innocent young woman and a child as casually as shooting trash-heap rats, their reckoning.

Earlier in the day, Hawk had lost the trail in the rain. It wasn't hard to figure where the jackals were heading, though. There weren't many trails in this neck of the rocky desert—at least, not many trails a white man dared follow and not end up slow-roasted over an Apache fire.

He put the grulla up a saddleback ridge and peered out through the separate streams funneling off his hat brim.

He wouldn't have to ride much farther.

Below, in a barren valley, on a low shelf under a high, anvil-shaped ridge, sat a small, two-story roadhouse, its two front windows and one side window lit against the stormy night. The frequent lightning flashes showed a pine-log hitching post out front, a sign over the brush arbor that Hawk couldn't read from this distance, and a small barn and corral on the right side of the trail.

Hawk reached back and shucked his Henry rifle from the saddle boot. The gun wolves had stopped here for the night. It was too wet to continue. Besides, they were wealthy men. Well-heeled hombres didn't sleep on the ground when they didn't have to. Especially when they had a pretty girl with them, and it was raining bear cubs and wolverines.

Hawk broke open the rifle's chamber, made sure he had a fresh shell seated, then raised the lever against the stock.

He rested the Henry over his saddle bows, lifted the collar of his yellow slicker, clucked to the horse, and headed slowly down the hill through the dripping saguaros that flashed like crucified martyrs on Cavalry Hill.

The wind and rain surged harder, turning the trail into a river, as he splashed down the ridge and halted the grulla between the corral and the barn. No horses milled behind the rails. They'd be in the barn for the night. In the road-house beyond, which the sign identified as Leo's Place, figures showed beyond the sashed, rain-streaked windows.

Hawk slid out of the saddle, opened the barn doors, and led the grulla inside. The trapped air was musty and warm with the smell of horses, hay, and manure. He closed the doors, found a lamp hanging with collars and harnesses on a four-by-four post, lit it, and held it aloft.

Copper eyes glistened in the lamplight, staring back at him from the rear shadows. Upon closer inspection, Hawk saw six stalled horses, all still damp. The tack piled on the stall partitions was also wet, the wool blankets hanging heavy on the pine planks.

Hawk tended the grulla, then checked the loads in his two pistols—a big Russian .44 positioned for the cross-draw on his left hip, and a stag-butted Colt on his right. He spun the Colt's cylinder, dropped the revolver in its holster, lowered his slicker over it, and grabbed his Henry, off-cocking the hammer.

He moved to the front of the barn, blew out the lamp, and opened the doors. He stood, letting his eyes range over the two-story cabin and stoop. The tang of burning mesquite cut through the slashing rain.

Thunder crashed like boulders. Lightning flashed ghostly blue.

Hawk pushed the doors closed and slogged through the mud to the front porch. He climbed the steps, setting each boot down softly, and tripped the door latch. The Z-frame door squawked inward, and he moved through it casually, doffing his hat and swiping it against his thigh.

The others in the room—five men playing cards or

checkers at two tables to his right, and the apron standing
behind the bar reading an illustrated newspaper spread
open on the pine planks to his left—shifted their eyes to
him.

Hawk didn't slip into even a crowded room unnoticed.
He was over six feet tall, broad-shouldered, and powerful
through the arms and shoulders. His father was a Ute war-
rior, his mother, a Norwegian immigrant's daughter. He
owned the thick, dark-brown hair and red-bronze skin of
his father, while his green, slanted eyes and high, tapering
cheekbones bespoke the Viking blood of his mother.

Under the slicker he wore a blue chambray shirt, red
neckerchief, sheepskin vest, and tight-fitting black denims.
His bench-made boots were plain brown and high-heeled,
the spurs unadorned.

The eyes stayed with him as he casually scraped mud
from his boots on the flour-sack rug inside the door, then
moved to the bar, his boots thumping hollowly against the
puncheons, spur chains ringing. He cast a quick glance
over the two groups of men sitting at two separate tables—
three at one table halfway down the room, two at another a
little farther back. The group of three was playing cards,
while the other two sat hunched over a checkerboard.

None had apparently scraped their boots, and dried mud
marked the floor around their chairs, telling Hawk they'd
been here a couple of hours.

One of the men at the first table, staring so hard at
Hawk as to bore holes through him, had long, stringy
blond hair, a red weasel face, and a big, hide-wrapped
bowie hanging down his chest from a leather lanyard.

The gang's segundo, Skylar Parks.

Upstairs, a man and a woman were talking. Must be the
top coyote himself, Shadow Nielsen. The woman must be
the banker's pretty daughter the gang had taken as a
hostage.

The barman, leaning on the pine planks, looked at the
five men at the tables, then shifted his brown eyes to Hawk.

His long, greasy hair hung down both sides of his pitted, blue-jowled face.

Straightening, he shook his hair back from his eyes. His voice betrayed a slight Irish accent. "Wet night to be out."

"I was glad to see your lights."

Hawk set the Henry's barrel on his right shoulder and turned sideways to the bar, glancing again at the unshaven, well-armed coyotes still regarding him sullenly through their tobacco smoke. Aside from the rain pounding the roof, the room was so quiet that Hawk's resonant voice sounded sepulchral in the close quarters.

"Got any coffee?"

"Not made."

"Whiskey, then. A bottle of something besides what you brew in the barn."

Before he'd finished the sentence, a sharp slap sounded above his head, in the second story. A man chuckled. Two seconds later, a girl giggled. Bedsprings squawked loudly.

Casting a furtive glance at the other customers, the barman chuckled as he reached under the bar. He set a brown, unlabeled bottle and a shot glass on the scarred planks. "Dollar and a quarter."

Hawk canted his head toward the five-gallon bucket at the end of the bar. "I'll take a couple of those hog knuckles, too."

As the bedsprings upstairs began squawking again, the man forked a couple knuckles out of the brine and set them on the planks before Hawk. The pork and vinegar smell made Hawk's stomach growl. He hadn't eaten since breakfast, and then only cold jerky and water.

"Three bits," the barman said.

Hawk flipped several coins onto the planks. Taking the knuckles in one hand, the bottle and his rifle in the other, he turned toward the room.

The coyotes were still staring at him through puffs of cigarette and cigar smoke. The second-in-command, Parks, sat back in his chair, holding a quirley between his thin, pink lips. He squinted through the smoke. His other hand rested negligently atop an ivory-butted Remington in a cross-draw holster. A sawed-off shotgun leaned against his chair.

His pinched face showed no expression.

The poker and the checkers had stalled. No one said anything. They smoked and stared at Hawk.

Upstairs, the bed squawked faster now, and the lovers groaned and sighed.

When Hawk's eyes had ranged across the room, his own face like granite, he moseyed over to a table near the smoking woodstove, set the bottle, knuckles, and glass on the table, then kicked out a chair. He laid the Henry across the table, angling it so the barrel pointed toward the middle of the small crowd before him, and shrugged out of his slicker.

He shook water from the oilskin, hung it over the back of a chair to his left, tossed his hat over the rifle's brass receiver, and sank down in the seat. It creaked loudly in the quiet room. A log in the woodstove fell.

Hawk sighed deeply and tipped the bottle over his shot glass, filling the glass to the brim. He set the bottle on the table and cast his gaze around the room, the coyotes still regarding him like a rabbit at a rattlesnake convention. The thought made the corners of his broad mouth twist up slightly.

He lifted the glass to the room, tossed it back.

The whiskey burned, instantly warming his chest and belly. Not bad coffin varnish for these parts.

Still keeping one eye on the glowering faces before him, Hawk lifted a hog knuckle, sniffed it, and took a bite. Vinegary and tough. It had sat in the brine too long and the hog had been old. Still, it tasted good to a hungry man just in from the rain.

He sat back in the chair, sipping his second shot and chewing the hog knuckle, staring blandly at the men glowering at him. The barman stood with his hands on the bar, a wing of hair hanging over one eye. The other eye was sharp with anxiety. He breathed heavily through his open mouth.

Hawk paid little attention to him. Hawk had never visited this corner of the Territory, but the place smelled and looked like an outlaw haunt. The barman, probably an old owlhoot himself, was no doubt in the habit of offering beds and whiskey to jaspers on the run.

Nevertheless, the barman was not Hawk's primary concern. Trouble, when it came, would come from the weasel-faced Skylar Parks, wanted in three territories and in Old Mexico for armed robbery and murder.

Upstairs, the mattress was getting a good workout, the headboard hammering the wall. It sounded like angry pistol shots. The man grunted and the woman sighed. Above Hawk's head, the ceiling creaked and groaned.

Hawk ripped another hunk of meat from the knuckle, washed it down with whiskey. Let Parks make the first move. Hawk could use the rest and the nourishment. Besides, he had all the time in the world.

Hawk finished the knuckle and dug in his shirt pocket for his makings sack. He'd begun rolling a smoke when Parks snorted and slid his chair back, the legs barking against the puncheons. Parks glanced at the other men, hitched up his gun belt, picked up his shotgun, and, holding the shotgun in one hand, sauntered toward Hawk.

Parks stopped as the headboard slammed one last, furious time against the wall, and the girl upstairs gave a shrill, deathlike exultation. The man groaned as though he'd run a mile to find the stage had already left the station.

Silence.

Parks continued toward Hawk, stopping five feet from Hawk's table. His sandy brows mantled his small, cobalt-blue eyes, and the mole to the left of his nose turned brick red. Hawk could smell the sweat-stink on him, the whiskey.

One hand on his pistol, the other holding the shotgun down near his thigh, finger on one of the two triggers, Parks spoke slowly. "Why the hell are you starin' at us?"

Hawk finished rolling his cigarette. When he licked it closed, he struck a match on the table, touched flame to the quirley. He took a deep drag.

Blowing smoke, he dipped his thumb and index finger into his shirt's left breast pocket, tossed a heavy copper star onto the table. It clanked and rolled, fell pin-down so that the words "Deputy U.S. Marshal" stared straight up at Parks.

"I've been sitting here trying to come up with a reason why I should take you boys in alive," Hawk said slowly, cigarette smoldering in his left hand. "And you know what?"

Parks's pupils expanded and contracted. "What?"

"I couldn't do it."

2.

HULLABALOO

PARKS blinked.

The air seemed to be sucked straight back behind him, as if the other coyotes were holding their collective breath.

Parks's upper lip curled as he took one step back. Raising the shotgun, he reached across his waist with his right hand, clawed the Remy from its holster, and, thumbing the hammer back, began swinging the barrel toward Hawk.

A revolver barked.

Parks winced and his right leg appeared to be jerked back as if by an unseen puppet string. The outlaw's face bleached as he screamed and, half-turning to his right, fired the shotgun and Remy into Hawk's table. The shotgun blast blew Hawk's whiskey bottle to smithereens, while the .44 slug plowed through a corner of the table and into the puncheons.

Having dived to his left after he'd fired his big Russian from under the table, Hawk lay on the floor on his left hip. He peered beneath the table at Parks's legs on the far side.

Parks's right knee was smoking as blood filled the .44 hole Hawk had drilled through the joint.

As Parks stumbled back, shrieking and cursing, Hawk loosed another shot from the silver-plated Russian, which sounded like a howitzer in the close quarters. A ragged .44 hole appeared in the inside of Parks's right thigh, sending his shrieks higher as he danced and pirouetted before the bar.

A pistol and a rifle barked at the same time as the other outlaws, gaining their feet, began flinging lead toward Hawk. Both slugs plowed into a chair on the far side of Hawk's ruined table. As another shot curled the air over his right ear and plunked into the wall behind him, Hawk threw the table over and ducked behind it.

Three shots popped through the flimsy pine, one tearing the nap from Hawk's right sleeve, one creasing the soft skin between the index and middle-finger knuckles of his right hand.

Hawk snaked his Russian and his Colt over the top edge of the table, peered into the shadows where the outlaws milled, sidestepping and aiming their revolvers and rifles, squinting through the smoke. As several more shots pealed around him, Hawk cut loose with both revolvers, pulling the triggers, cocking the hammers, pulling the triggers again. He sent two men dancing back and falling over tables, while another dropped his Colt Navy and clutched his arm.

"Son of a *bitch*!"

As the man lowered his head toward his chest, another slug plunked through the top of his hat. He jerked and collapsed.

Hawk lowered his head but continued firing the Russian and the Colt until both hammers clicked empty. Then he dropped both guns, bolted to his feet, and leapt the overturned table. As he scooped his Henry off the floor, he cast a glance into the smoky shadows, where the surviving outlaws milled, out of sight behind chairs and their own overturned tables.

One man fired from behind the woodstove, but the slug plowed through the room's center post a good five feet ahead and to the right of Hawk. Hawk dropped to a knee, thumbed the Henry's hammer back, and fired. The broad forehead of the man peeking around the stove turned pink as he gave a startled grunt and fell back against the wall, flapping his arms as if trying to fly.

A big bear of a man with two salt-and-pepper braids and an eye patch heaved to his feet from behind a table, and fired a Starr .44 in each hand. Hawk threw himself right and rolled off his right shoulder as both slugs plunked into the pail of hog knuckles atop the bar.

Hawk rose to a crouch, levering a fresh shell into the Henry's breech, snapping the butt to his shoulder, and firing two quick rounds.

The man screamed, eyes snapping wide as, both smoking pistols held straight out before him, he glanced down at the two holes in his chest—perfectly parallel and spaced three inches apart, directly over his heart.

In the corner of Hawk's left eye, someone moved. A fierce, defiant shriek rose as a pistol flashed through the smoke and murky lantern light.

Hawk swiveled right and ran, taking three strides and then lofting himself over the bar. Three bullets, fast as wind-driven hail, popped into the cracked mirror behind the bar above his head. Hawk smashed into the back wall and hit the floor on his right shoulder and hip.

Ahead, the barman crouched, knees drawn to his chest. He lifted his head from his arms, hair hanging like strings around his face, eyes bright with fear. "What a goddamn hullabaloo—look what you done to my place!"

Hawk raked another shell into the Henry. "Not finished yet."

The scream came again, followed by a string of Spanish epithets. Peering out from under the bar, Hawk saw a swarthy man in a steeple-crowned, straw sombrero stagger toward him, kicking fallen chairs and tables out of his way.

To Hawk's right, half under a table, Parks grunted and groaned, a pool of blood growing beneath his ruined legs.

The Mexican emerged from the smoke and shadows, a bracket lamp revealing a round, mustachioed face with bright, black eyes set beneath sloping brows. The man held a hand to his bloody belly. Blood dribbled down from the left corner of his mouth and between the three or four teeth in his lower jaw.

"Sangre de Cristo, usted me mato!" Blood of Christ, you killed me.

He raised the pistol, cracked off another shot. The slug barked into the floor a foot in front of Hawk. The shooter triggered the gun again but the hammer clicked, empty.

As the Mexican tossed away the spent Schofield and grabbed a second gun from behind his horsehide sash, Hawk scurried over to the beer keg to his right, which held up one end of the three cottonwood planks composing the bar. The second Schofield popped twice, one shot chunking into the floor in front of the keg, the other into the keg itself, which jerked against Hawk's left shoulder.

The Mexican's boots thumped toward the bar, spurs chinging. The Mexican was sobbing and cursing in Spanish.

"Shit," the barman said, throwing himself flat on the floor. "Ah, shit, shit, shit . . ."

Hawk glanced at him. "You're awfully grim." He threw himself right, out from behind the keg, and onto his elbows, raising the Henry in both hands. The Mexican stood five feet from the bar, lifting his enraged eyes to peer over the top.

Hawk fired. The Mexican jerked toward him, and the slug merely sliced the lobe from the Mexican's left ear.

The Mexican fired the Schofield. The bullet sliced through the top of Hawk's left arm. Gritting his teeth, Hawk rose to his knees.

As the Mexican raised his Schofield's barrel and thumbed the hammer back, ignoring the blood pouring from his ear, Hawk rammed another shell into the Henry's breech, the spent casing smoking across his right shoulder and hitting the floor with a ping.

Teetering like a windmill in a prairie twister, the Mexican canted the Schofield toward Hawk and fired a half second before Hawk levered two rounds through each of the man's sun-seared cheeks, and one through his heart. The Mexican's own slug plowed into the base of the wall behind Hawk.

The Mexican—punched straight back and lifted off his feet—was dead before he hit the floor.

Hawk levered another round and peered through the wafting smoke. The smell of cordite was tempered by the smell of brine still dribbling to the floor in two streams from the bucket of hog knuckles. Around the demolished room, nothing moved. The five men were down, twisted amidst the rubble.

Silence except for the twin streams of brine dribbling onto the floor, and the sharp, anguished breaths of Skylar Parks, lying under a broken table ten feet away from Hawk and staring at the ceiling. Rain still lashed the walls and windows, and wan lightning flashed, but the storm's fury had passed.

Behind Hawk, wood creaked. He threw himself right as a pistol popped twice.

He hit the floor on his butt and raised the Henry toward the stairs at the back of the room. A mustachioed face peered out through the rails near the top of the staircase. A silver-plated gun barrel angled toward Hawk, who fired two rounds. The slugs hammered through a rail support on both sides of the mustachioed gent's face.

Shadow Nielsen cursed, withdrew the gun, and bolted the three steps to the top of the stairs.

Hawk turned toward the bar. The barman was still down on all fours, hands laced across the back of his head, his forehead pressed to the floor.

"There a back way out of this place?" Hawk asked.

The barman lifted his head, looked around warily, then slid his gaze to Hawk. He shook his head.

Hawk stood and set his rifle atop the bar. He probably had two or three rounds left in the long gun. He walked back to his broken table, picked up the Russian and the Colt, and loaded both at the bar, thumbing cartridges from the leather loops on his shell belt.

The ceiling creaked. Hushed, agitated voices rose in the second story.

Hawk spun the Russian's cylinder, then picked up the Colt. Holding each gun down low at his sides, he started toward the stairs. He paused over Skylar Parks.

The outlaw's rheumy blue eyes, glazed with shock from blood loss and fear, met Hawk's. "I'm gonna . . . I'm gonna need a doctor real bad," he croaked.

Hawk stared down at him, shook his head. "Undertaker, you mean."

Hawk aimed the Colt at Parks's forehead. Parks stared up at the revolver's barrel, eyes crossing. He'd started shaping his mouth for an exclamation, his eyes snapping wide, when the Colt barked.

The slug drilled through the middle of Parks's forehead, where the veins above his nose forked. His mouth opened and closed several times, his boots shaking. Then his open eyes turned to marbles, and he lay still.

"Christ!" exclaimed the bartender, standing at the far end of the bar, shaking his head.

"Dirty job," Hawk said, moving toward the stairs. "Somebody's gotta do it."

Hawk stopped at the bottom of the narrow stairs, peering up to the second-story landing. Nothing up there but a framed print of a plump, naked blonde spread out like a female smorgasbord on pink satin sheets in a jungle. A lantern guttered on the wall above the railing.

Hawk climbed the stairs slowly, his boots making the steps squawk, the spurs chiming softly.

Two steps from the top, he stopped, thumbed the hammers of both revolvers back, and edged a peek around the corner. The dim hall was empty.

Hawk turned into it. A musty runner ran the length of

the hall. It cushioned Hawk's heels as he strode slowly between the walls of bald, vertical cottonwood planks. Two bracket lamps shunted circular shadows across the walls. Their wicks had not been trimmed, and the black smoke hung like fog beneath the ceiling. The air smelled like coal oil and sex.

The door of the last room on the left was open. Soft, red light angled from it.

A man stepped out of the room, blocking the light. Holding a woman before him, he stood facing Hawk at the end of the hall, before a low, sashed window through which distant lightning flashed.

Hawk stopped, aiming both pistols straight out from his shoulders.

Shadow Nielsen had dressed hurriedly. His hair hung uncombed from beneath his big plainsman hat, and his shirttails hung over his cartridge belt and black denim trousers. Two sets of saddlebags, two pockets stuffed with clothes, were looped over his left shoulder.

The girl before him—a small, thin brunette—was clad in a see-through nightgown, her arms and legs bare. She stood stiffly before Nielsen, brown eyes riveted on Hawk, as Nielsen held his silver-plated .45 to her jaw.

"Drop it," Nielsen barked. "Or she dies."

Hawk blinked, kept the revolver leveled. "Kill her."

Nielsen squinted one eye. The girl frowned slightly.

"I'm warnin' you," Nielsen said. "I ain't just dancin' with this pretty little banker's daughter. I *will* kill her if you don't put those guns down and back away." He cocked the .45's hammer. "You wanna take her pretty little *carcass* back to her daddy?"

"Why not?" Hawk growled. "I don't reckon her daddy would have much use for a little tramp that ran off with the men who robbed his bank."

"Ran *off*?" the girl said, indignant. She shifted her bare feet on the runner, her breasts jouncing behind the nightgown. "I didn't have a choice. They took me out of my father's office."

"Maybe you were in your old man's office because you knew Nielsen was comin'. Maybe you figured your old man would be more likely to turn over the combination to the safe if he thought his daughter's life was imperiled." Hawk paused and leveled his gaze at Nielsen. "Go ahead and kill her. Then face me like a man."

Nielsen's chest rose and fell sharply. The girl beetled her brows, and her cheeks turned crimson.

"I'm warnin' you, lawman." Nielsen pressed the .45's barrel hard against her jaw. "I'm callin' your bluff!"

The girl winced and slid her fearful eyes toward Nielsen as he gripped her tighter around the neck. "Shadow . . . don't . . ."

Hawk smiled down the long barrel of his Russian .44.

"I'm gonna kill this little bitch!" Nielsen's voice boomed around the hall. "I ain't gonna warn you again. You don't drop those hoglegs in three seconds, I'm gonna blow her fucking *head off*!"

The girl's eyes snapped wide. She bunched her lips and squirmed, trying to wrench herself free of the big man's grasp. "Shadow, let me *go*!" She bit his left hand.

"Ouch!" Nielsen's thick arm jerked away from the girl, and she spun toward the wall, getting her feet entangled with Nielsen's boots and falling, hands slapping the cottonwood planks. "Ivy, you fuckin' bitch!"

The saddlebags tumbling from his shoulder, Nielsen lashed out at her, stopped, and turned to Hawk grinning down the Russian's barrel at the outlaw leader. Nielsen's eyes flashed fear as he jerked his Colt up.

Hawk's Russian leapt in his hand. *Pop!*

The Colt spoke. *Ka-paw! Ka-paw!*

Then the Russian again: *Pop, pop, pop!*

The thick powder smoke wafted around Hawk's head, making his eyes burn. He slitted his lids and peered at the end of the hall. Nielsen stood straight back against the wall, against the window, arms hanging slack at his sides. Blood fountained from the four holes in his chest, spraying the girl cowering on the floor to his right.

She screamed and hid her face in her arms and raised knees.

Nielsen's Colt slipped out of his hand, hitting the floor with a thud. He sighed, eyes rolling back in his head. Then he sagged down to the floor and lowered his chin to his chest. After a few seconds, he rolled onto a shoulder, his blood pooling around him.

Hawk lowered his revolvers and strode down the hall. He glanced at the girl sobbing into her blood-splashed arms. He picked up Nielsen's pistol from the blood pool, emptied it, letting the cartridges clink to the floor, then tossed the revolver into the darkened room, skidding it under the bed.

He fished around in Nielsen's saddlebags. When he found the set with the money the gang had stolen from the bank and the Wells Fargo office—over ten thousand dollars of bundled greenbacks—he slung the bags over his shoulder and turned again to the girl.

"You best split ass for home." Hawk adjusted the saddlebags on his shoulder. "Before I take you over my knee."

She lifted her head, her cheeks tear-streaked. "I'll never go back there. I hate that town and those boring people!"

"Well, you best go somewhere. You've worn out your welcome in these parts."

The girl cried in her arms as Hawk walked away down the hall and descended the stairs.

3

TWO HALVES OF A DEAD RAT

DOWNSTAIRS, Hawk slung the Henry and the saddlebags onto one of the few standing tables. The bartender stood trimming the wick of a coal-oil lamp that hadn't been shattered in the hullabaloo, sweat glistening on his cheeks.

His anxious eyes followed Hawk. "All in a night's work, huh?" he groused.

Hawk moved behind the bar. He took a bottle and a beer mug from separate shelves and half-filled the mug with whiskey. He corked the bottle, returned it to the shelf, then picked up the mug and walked back to his table.

He sat down heavily, taking a deep drink from the mug.

On the other side of the room, the barman cursed as he looked around the room littered with ruined furniture and mangled bodies. He sighed, opened the front door, and walked over to where Parks lay beneath an overturned table, staring sightlessly up at the ceiling. The barman stooped, grabbed Parks's ankles, and began dragging the dead outlaw toward the front door.

As the man dragged a second body toward the door, he stopped and regarded Hawk with beetled brows. "You could lend me a hand, 'stead of sittin' there swillin' my whiskey!"

Hawk had crossed his boots on a chair. Now he removed them and stood. "You gave the skunks sanctuary. Endure the stench." He grabbed his rifle and the money-stuffed saddlebags from the table. "I'm going to bed."

He picked up the beer mug, turned, and headed for the stairs. Behind him, the barman cursed and continued dragging the dead Mexican toward the door.

As Hawk mounted the second-story landing, he saw the girl still sitting where he'd left her, head in her hands. She was no longer sobbing. She just sat there. Hawk chuffed, opened the door of the first room on the left, went inside, and closed the door softly behind him.

Five hours later, Hawk opened the door and stepped into the hall, a long, slender Lobo Negro cigar protruding from between his lips. He carried his Henry in his right hand, the saddlebags draped over his left shoulder. His sheepskin vest was buttoned halfway up his chest, and his revolvers rode high on his hips. The thick, dark-brown hair hanging down from his broad-brimmed black hat was damp from the water he'd brushed through it with his hands.

Hawk glanced to his left, where the sashed window at the end of the hall shone with milky blue light. The girl was gone. Nielsen's body was gone, too, and the blood scrubbed up, but a large smudge remained. It looked like oil in the murky light.

Hawk descended the stairs to the main room. The bartender sat at one of the three remaining tables, crouched over a plate, forking eggs and side pork into his mouth. A lamp burned on the bar, but the room was mostly in shadow.

"The place looks damn near civilized," Hawk said as he fired his cigar from the lamp cylinder.

The bartender shoved another forkful into his mouth and slid his chair back. He gestured to the chair across from him. "Have a seat. I'll be right back."

Drawing on the Lobo Negro, Hawk watched the barman disappear through a curtained doorway behind the bar. Hawk blew out a long smoke plume, sauntered over to the table, slung the saddlebags and rifle over a chair, and sat down.

Presently, the barman reappeared, a steaming tin plate in one hand, a steaming stone mug in the other. He set both before Hawk. The plate was piled with scrambled eggs, two fatty chunks of side pork, and toast still smoking from the range top, basted with butter. The coffee looked rich and black.

Hawk arched a brow at the barman smiling across the table at him. "I'm gonna have to wreck your place more often."

The barman snickered and shook a shock of stringy hair back from his left eye. As Hawk picked up his fork and dug into the eggs, the barman reached into his left breast pocket and flipped Hawk's copper star onto the table. Hawk glanced at it, then at the barman smiling at him like the cat that ate the canary.

"Found that when I was cleanin' up."

"Obliged." Hawk picked up the badge, ran his thumb across the engraved words, "Deputy U.S. Marshal," then stuffed it into his own shirt pocket and returned to his food.

He'd eaten half when the barman finished his own plate and, taking his mug in both hands, leaned back in his chair. "For a cut of that lucre—a very small cut—you won't have nothin' to worry about."

Hawk stopped his fork halfway to his mouth, glanced across the table. The barman hooded his eyes knowingly. "I won't say a word about you takin' those boys down without givin' 'em a chance to give themselves up *first*."

"I'm not worried about it." Hawk shoved the fork into his mouth, then took up his knife and cut off a chunk of side pork. The barman continued staring at him, squeezing his coffee mug in his dark hands.

Finally, the man leaned forward in his chair as if, though he and Hawk were probably the only two people within thirty square miles, he might be overheard. "Be a sport. That's a lot of money." He glanced at the bulging pouches to his right. "You're gonna take a cut. Give me a little . . . for wreckin' my place if nothin' else."

"You have six good mustangs in your barn, and you took the guns off the bodies, didn't you?" Hawk stared at him. "And probably a couple hundred dollars from their pockets?"

The man's cheeks balled. "But, shit, that's a lot of lucre!"

Hawk chewed a hunk of side pork and sipped his coffee. "It's going back to Cartridge Springs. Every penny."

The barman glared, mouth half-open. "Bullshit!"

"Every penny."

When Hawk finished his plate, he threw back the last of his coffee and picked his cold cigar up from the table. Standing and slinging the saddlebags over his shoulder and taking the Henry in his right hand, he moved to the bar and relit the cheroot at the lamp.

"Obliged for the breakfast," he told the barman as he strode toward the door, puffing smoke.

Behind Hawk, the barman's chair scraped across the puncheons. "Hey, wait a damn minute!"

Hawk grabbed his oilskin off a wall hook and kept moving through the door, down the porch steps, and across the soggy yard. Behind him, the barman's raspy, Irish-accented voice rose. "You're that crazy lawman from the Plains, ain't ye? The one that went loco when some outlaw hanged your boy—"

Hawk stopped and half-turned, his shaggy dark brows mantling his ice-green eyes.

The barman grinned, his stringy hair shading his face. "Sure as shit."

Hawk hefted his rifle and continued toward the barn. "Hey!" the barman shouted. "They's been people lookin' fer you!"

Hawk continued walking, boots crunching softly in the damp gravel. He stared at the dark barn looming in the cool, gray dawn, the sky lightening behind it. But in his mind's eye, young Jubal hung from a cottonwood tree atop a high hill . . . his small, plump body swinging in the lashing rain while lightning danced around him.

"*No!*" Hawk had shouted.

But he'd been too late. By the time he'd cut him down, the boy was dead. And Three-Fingers Ned Meade was riding down the other side of the hill, him and his gang disappearing in the stormy darkness.

Hawk jerked the left door open and disappeared inside, leaving the door half-open behind him. Ten minutes later, the door flew wide and Hawk reappeared from the barn's inner shadows, leading his saddled grulla. His rifle was in his saddle boot, and his oilskin was wrapped around his bedroll.

The fiery grulla pranced and tossed its head, eager to hit the trail.

The barman was still standing on the porch, one hand on an awning post. "There's been a man around, lookin' fer you."

Hawk had grabbed the saddle horn and had turned out a stirrup. He stopped and stretched a glance toward the roadhouse, the bulky barman silhouetted against the open front door.

"That ain't news to me."

"This one wasn't no bounty hunter. A lawman, he was." The barman traced a small circle on his chest and stretched his lips back from his teeth. "Big copper star, just like yours."

"He have a handle?"

"Flagg. Had six others with him, all wearin' stars. Said they had a warrant from four Territorial governors. A *death* warrant. Made out just for you." The barman rose up on the toes of his worn, low-heeled boots, his grin showing wider. "Said it was my duty as a U.S. citizen to report any encounter I might have with this man they was lookin' for . . . this Gideon Henry Hawk. Vigilante lawman from the Plains."

Hawk turned, grabbed his saddle horn, toed a stirrup, and swung into the saddle. He neck-reined the grulla toward the roadhouse. The barman stared at Hawk riding toward him, the smile slowly fading from the Irishman's thin, chapped lips. He removed his hand from the awning post and took a single, slow step back.

Hawk turned the grulla sideways to the porch and favored the man with a level stare. "If Flagg comes through here again, tell him to go home." He shook his head. "I don't cotton to killing lawmen, but any man running up my backside dies, lawman or no."

Hawk slapped his holster, a blur of fluid movement. Then the Colt was in his hand, cocked and shoulder high, aimed at the roadhouse.

The barman screamed, crossing his arms in front of his face and bolting straight back.

The Colt barked, echoing around the morning-quiet yard.

The barman tripped over his own feet, falling hard on his rump. Rolling his fear-bright eyes around in their sockets, he slowly lowered his hands. To his right, in the far corner of the open roadhouse door, a large rat lay in two bloody halves.

He turned to Hawk. The big lawman was riding away from him, heading for the eastern trail and the saddleback ridge, broad shoulders sloping under the sheepskin vest.

"Best not leave your door open," Hawk called over his right shoulder. "Or next thing, you'll be giving sanctuary to rats."

Three days later, under cover of darkness, Hawk rode into the foothills town of Cartridge Springs, a ranching burg in the central Territory. It was Saturday, and ranch hands were whooping it up along the main street, gas lamps and firebrands illuminating the false-fronted saloons and hotels like dance halls in hell.

Hawk asked one of the pie-eyed drovers stumbling across the street where he would find the bank president's home. Five minutes later, he dismounted his grulla at the dark south end of the village, under a sprawling cottonwood.

The breeze rustled the leaves, and crickets chirped. In the distance, a dog yipped at coyotes yammering in the hills.

Ground-tying the horse, Hawk slung the saddlebags stuffed with greenbacks over his shoulder and crept through the shadows before a large stone house with a well-tended yard surrounded by a white picket fence.

Several windows were lit, and a piano pattered inside. It didn't sound like the banker was pining overmuch for his daughter.

Quietly, eyeing the curtained first-story windows, Hawk turned through the gate, strode up the brick walk, and mounted the porch. He dropped the saddlebags on a wicker rocking chair, rapped twice on the door, then turned and strode out of the yard, latching the gate and mounting his horse.

When he rode back to the main drag, he stabled the grulla and, his saddlebags over his shoulder and his rifle in his hand, went looking for the quietest hotel in town.

He found it on a side street—two stories of sun-blistered pine, only three horses and a mule tethered to the hitch rack, and two middle-aged men in conservative suits sipping beers on the porch. The place was as dark as a funeral parlor, only one downstairs window softly lit.

As Hawk strode toward a spot at the hitch rack between a horse and a mule, he stopped suddenly, then wheeled, raising his rifle one-handed. His neck hairs were prickling, as though someone were watching him . . . following him.

His gaze swept the opposite side of the street, where a few shanties and a couple of wood-frame shops hunkered in the sage and broom grass, starlight smeared in their windows. Hawk eyed a rain barrel near the left front corner of one shanty. A sudden wind gust swept dirt along the street. Behind the hovels, a cat moaned.

Otherwise, nothing moved. The only sound was the cat,

the muffled din of the reveling ranch hands, and the desultory voices of the two men on the hotel stoop.

Inside, Hawk asked the white-haired gent behind the desk for a room and signed the register.

"For only one extra dollar, I'll send a girl up."

Hawk squinted at the bug-eyed oldster in his crisp white shirt and hand-knit vest, a bow tie snugged against the old man's turkey neck.

The night clerk shrugged, and his swivel chair squeaked. "I gotta compete with the hotels on Main. I can send for a girl from Miss De Voe's across the way. Like I said, it's only one extra dollar, and I hear tell those gals really know their work." He closed a moth-wing lid over one bulging blue eye. "Not a one over eighteen!"

Hawk plucked the key from the register book. "Next time."

He mounted the stairs at the rear of the lobby, found his room, washed, undressed, climbed into the brass-framed bed, blew out the lamp, and let his head sink back on the pillow.

He wasn't sure how much time had passed before he opened his eyes. He'd heard something.

The lamp was lit, casting soft yellow light and shadows. Warm, sweet breath pushed against his face. He jerked his head back, snapped a hand toward his gun belt coiled over a bedpost, clawed the Russian from the holster, and clicked the hammer back.

A woman laughed and leapt back from the bed. "Easy, lover! It's me, Saradee Jones."

She laughed again. When Hawk's eyes focused, he saw the heart-shaped face framed in billowing, copper-colored hair.

The heart-stopping, high-breasted, round-hipped body, clad in only a dusty trail hat and a flimsy chemise . . .

4.

NIGHT VISITOR

HAWK blinked at the gorgeous, near-naked woman standing before his bed, her full red lips stretched back from her teeth, blue eyes flashing devilishly in the lamplight.

He had to be dreaming. His senses were as keen as a cougar's. No one could sneak into his room, light a lamp, and undress without him hearing.

Saradee Jones stepped toward the bed, putting her bare feet down softly, gently shoving his cocked pistol aside with the back of her left hand and then sitting down beside him, making the bedsprings squawk. She'd been reading his mind. Her tone was vaguely cajoling.

"You must've been riding hard, last few days. Didn't think I could sneak into your room, much less light a lamp while you snored like a drunken sailor." She leaned down and kissed his cheek. "You're getting careless, Mr. Hawk."

Hawk pushed her back with one hand, aimed the cocked Russian at her with the other. "What the hell are you doing here?" He scowled, brows beetling. "How in the hell did you get in here?"

"Skeleton key." She hefted her magnificent breasts.

"The old man downstairs went soft as fresh cow plop when I thrust these in his face."

"I told you next time I saw you, I'd kill you."

Chuckling, she leaned forward, her left hand nudging his pistol up into the deep crease between her breasts. The sheer chemise drew taut against the orbs, revealing their fullness and roundness, each separately defined, the nipples jutting against the fabric. She ran her fingertips along the gun's barrel, then down along his hand and wrist, tickling him with her nails. "Why don't you fire?"

Hawk glared at her, his trigger finger tensing.

He should shoot her. Her death would be no loss. She was a thief and a killer, her gang having wiped out nearly an entire detachment of an army payroll guard before Hawk had tracked her to Mexico last year. Everywhere she went, she piled up the bodies of men who fell prey to her charms.

A priestess as dark and cunning as Lorelei, she was more depraved than she was beautiful.

Hawk swallowed, eased the tension in his trigger finger.

But there was no denying that she *was* beautiful . . . and the most alluring, sensuous creature he'd ever known. As much as he wanted to squeeze the Russian's trigger, something stopped him.

His heart drummed in his ears.

He raised the barrel, depressed the hammer, set the revolver on the dresser beside the bed, and grabbed her arms, pulling her to him harshly. He kissed her. She drew back slightly, keeping her forehead pressed to his, stretching her lips back from her teeth, chuckling.

"I knew you couldn't do it!"

He brought his right hand up and wrapped his fingers around her neck. He stared into her eyes, the pupils contracting slightly with fear as the color rose in her cheeks.

He bunched his lips, his own cheeks flushing with anger, but then he loosened his grip and pulled her down toward him. She sucked a breath, closed her lips over her teeth, and, groaning, threw her arms around him, mashing her mouth down on his.

He reached behind her, took the back of the chemise in his hands, and ripped it with one, passionate thrust. He flung the garment to the floor, rose up on his elbows, and rolled Saradee over onto her back.

She cried out in ecstasy as he rose up on his hands and thrust himself between her legs. He stopped, stared bemusedly down at her. She moaned and wrapped her ankles around his back, bouncing her butt. "Please . . . please . . ."

He squeezed her breast with his right hand, leaned down, and closed his mouth over hers, kissing her savagely as he rose up then thrust down once more.

She convulsed and bucked beneath him, locking her ankles behind his back and sucking his tongue more deeply into her.

He placed his fists on either side of her head, leaning on his arms and pummeling her with his hips until the bed-springs sounded like a steam engine on a fast downgrade.

Later, he lay back on his pillow, one hand behind his head. Saradee lay naked beside him, resting her head on his shoulder, combing the auburn hair on his chest with her fingers, her breasts feeling soft and warm against his side.

"You got no cause to look so sour," she said, glancing into his pensive green eyes fixed on the ceiling. "I have as much cause to kill you as you, me."

"How the hell do you figure that?"

She curled her lip and gave a couple of his chest hairs a tug. "You used me, you bastard. Pretended to throw in with me and my boys. You stole back the payroll money, foiled our attempt to take the Mexican gold, and . . . hmmm, hmmm, what else? Oh, yes, now I remember . . . you *killed off my entire gang*!"

"Butchers, all. Including you."

"Don't be uppity. You're not exactly an altar boy." She snugged her cheek against his neck, ran her hand, fingers splayed, across his flat belly, stretching the tips of her fingers below his waist. "You and I could raise hob, if we threw in together."

Hawk chuffed. "Forget it."

She ran the hand lower and canted her eyes up toward his. "We could have all kinds of fun . . . make a ton of money. I've got a new gang startin' up. Old friends, you might say. Those boys could use a ramrod to give 'em some direction. I could use a good ramrod, my ownself." Her hand tightened around him. "Come on, Hawk. You're more like me than you think. You could have shot me a few minutes ago. Instead . . . well . . . you know . . ."

Her hand was doing what she'd intended. Hawk cursed, flung the quilt and her hand aside, and crawled out of bed. Naked, he padded over to the chair where Saradee's two Colts were wrapped in their cartridge belt.

He shucked one of the guns. Reclining on an elbow, her rose-tipped breasts slanting toward the bed, Saradee watched him uncertainly.

Hawk opened the loading gate and emptied the cylinder onto the floor. The bullets clinked and rolled. When he'd unloaded the other gun in the same fashion, he shoved both back into their holsters.

"Don't trust me?"

"Your reputation precedes you."

She'd brought a bottle. He grabbed it off the washstand, popped the cork, and took a long swig. He set the bottle back on the stand, walked back to the bed, and sat on the edge.

"How long you been trailin' me?"

She shrugged. "A couple days."

He reached out, slid a lock of copper-colored hair away from her face with the back of his hand, hooked it behind her ear. His voice was at once soft and firm. "You keep doggin' me, I will kill you."

Holding his gaze, her eyes flashed with tiny javelins. "I wouldn't blame you," she said, just above a whisper, keeping her eyes on his. She turned slowly onto her right shoulder, pulled the pillow down to her hips, and turned onto it, lying breasts-down against the sheets. She lifted her head, threw her hair back, adjusted the pillow with her thighs, and stuck her round, pink rump in the air.

"I wouldn't blame you a bit." She sighed and lay her cheek on the sheet. "Kill me once more tonight, lover. Then we'll see who kills who next time we meet."

United States Territorial Marshal D.W. "Dutch" Flagg strode along the south side of the main street in Cartridge Springs, hat pulled down over his forehead, boots pounding the boardwalk, arms swinging stiffly at his sides.

Flagg's gray brows were furrowed over his wide-set eyes, and his cheeks above his thin, gray beard were brick red—a product of the chill morning wind and a lifelong weakness for brandy.

As a particularly cold gust whistled between the false fronts, Flagg winced and raised the collar of his corduroy jacket against his neck. Snagging an empty whiskey bottle with his boot toe, skidding it off down the walk, Flagg stopped before the St. Louis Hotel.

The main window was dark, but a light shone in the back. The St. Louis didn't look like Hawk's kind of digs, but it was worth a try.

Habitually brushing his hand against the walnut-gripped Remington holstered under his jacket, the lawman reached for the door handle. Someone whistled, barely audible beneath the breeze.

Flagg stopped and peered up the street. Three men stood in the middle of a crossroads one block west, facing Flagg, all wearing dusters, two holding Winchesters across their chests, the third with a double-bore shotgun. Their copper badges flashed in the faint, predawn light.

One of the deputies canted his head toward a cross street and beckoned to Flagg.

Flagg glanced over his right shoulder. A half block away, on the other side of the street, three more deputies were walking along the opposite boardwalk. Flagg beckoned to the men, then stepped off the boardwalk and headed for the three at the crossroads.

"What?" Flagg said as he approached deputies Miller, Villard, and Tuttle.

Miller spat a tobacco quid. "A freighter told us he seen a man matching Hawk's description headed for the Saguaro Hotel yonder."

"Saw," Flagg said with a self-righteous sneer.

Miller slitted an eye. "What?"

Flagg shook his head with disgust. "He *saw* a man headed for the hotel. You're senior deputy, Miller. Please learn to talk like one."

Flagg wheeled, jerked his head at the three approaching deputies, and headed up the cross street. Behind him, Miller glanced at Villard.

"Contrary cuss, ain't he?"

Villard snorted and started after Flagg. "A man who's set his hat for the governor's office can't 'sociate with men who say *seen* when they shoulda said *saw*." He glanced over his shoulder. "Dummy."

"Yeah," Miller sneered, half a step behind Villard. "You Cajuns talk *real* good."

At the head of the pack of deputies, Flagg approached the Saguaro Hotel. He mounted the stoop, and, hand on his pistol butt, opened the front door. Flagg stepped into the misty-dark lobby, boot thuds cushioned by a thick rug, and looked around cautiously as he headed for the front desk.

To his left, flanked by a potted palm, a wizened oldster with thin gray hair sat in an overstuffed easy chair, head thrown back, lower jaw sagging. A big, tortoiseshell cat slept on the old man's left thigh, sphinxlike, while silver-framed spectacles rested on the man's other knee.

The oldster snored softly. A clock ticked woodenly, accenting the predawn silence.

Flagg crossed to the man, looked down as the other deputies ranged out in a semicircle behind him, holding their rifles and shotguns in both hands and glancing at the stairs.

The cat leapt to the floor with an indignant trill, then disappeared through a door flanking the front desk. The old man's eyes snapped wide. He opened his mouth, but before he could say anything, Flagg pressed a finger to his lips.

The man stared bug-eyed at the gray-bearded lawman, his rheumy eyes warily sweeping the well-armed deputies behind him.

Hand still resting on his pistol butt and stretching a cautious gaze toward the staircase, stray light glistening on the varnished mahogany, Flagg spoke softly. "You have a man registered here—big man with green eyes and dark-brown hair. Wears a black hat and a sheepskin vest." Flagg arched a silver brow at the old man. "Correct?"

The old man donned his glasses, folding the bows back behind his pouch-lobed, red ears. "The man sure gets a lot o' company."

"Who else?"

"Woman came in last night. Said she was a friend."

"Whore?"

"Wasn't painted up, but then, I don't keep up with the fashions." The old man snorted. "Wore two guns on her waist, like Calamity Jane Canary. Rather . . . uh . . . bold young lady."

"She still up there?"

"Far as I know. I reckon I nodded off."

Flagg glanced at Villard and Miller on his left, then switched his gaze to the stairs rising into the second-story shadows. Without looking at the old man, he said, "Which room?"

"Six."

Flagg drew a breath and moved toward the stairs. "Obliged." At the bottom of the stairs, he stopped and, stooping to grab the heel of his left boot, turned to the others. "Take off your boots."

J.C. Garth grunted, "Huh?"

"The man has eyes like an eagle and ears like a wildcat. Off with the boots. Once we're on the stairs, no talking. Not even whispering. Communicate by gesture only."

The men struggled out of their boots, each grunting and stumbling around on one foot. Garth set a boot down beside the newel post. The spur chinged softly.

Flagg shot him a hard look. "Shhh!"

Garth froze, wincing. "Sorry."

When they were all out of their boots and had quietly levered shells into their rifle breeches or eared their shotguns' hammers back, they mounted the stairs behind Flagg. The lead lawman moved slowly, lifting one stockinged foot at a time and pointing his cocked pistol straight up the dark stairs.

They crabbed along the dim hall to room six. Three deputies flanking him on each side, Flagg listened at the door, then stepped back, nodding at the largest deputy, Avery "Hound-Dog" Tuttle. The deputy, who weighed nearly two thirty in his birthday suit, hefted his shotgun and stepped three feet back from the door.

He looked at Flagg. Flagg nodded.

Tuttle lowered his head, dug his thin white socks into the rug, and bulled ahead, throwing his right shoulder forward.

The shoulder smashed into the door with a crunching boom.

Wood splinters and the iron latch flew from the frame as the door burst inward, and Hound-Dog disappeared inside.

5.

INTERROGATION

HOLDING his Remington straight out from his shoulder, Flagg strode into the room, turning toward the bed on his right. The other five deputies scrambled in behind him, aiming their rifles and shotgun.

To Flagg's left, Hound-Dog was down on one knee, hatless, aiming his greener at the bed, breathing hard.

Flagg held his gaze on the bed's far side. A single, slender figure lay beneath quilts. At the head of the bed, copper-colored hair shone, and two blue eyes burned through shadows at Flagg.

The woman's voice was taut with fury. "Who the hell are you?"

Flagg's eyes went to the pillow to the girl's right, still hollowed where a head had lain. He craned his neck to rake his gaze around the room, then returned his eyes to the girl.

"Where's Hawk?"

She glanced at the pillow beside her. Then her eyes, too, ran a quick sweep of the room. "Haven't seen no one called Hawk."

Flagg stepped toward her, aiming his revolver at her forehead. "He was here last night. When did he leave?"

She scuttled up in the bed, rested her back against the headboard. The manuever left her magnificent breasts bare for a second, before she raised a quilt to her neck and curled her lip at Flagg. "I don't know anyone called Hawk. I spent the night alone. Now, I'm waiting for your apology, mister, and for you and your limp-dicked tin stars to haul your asses the hell out of my room."

"He's registed downstairs." Flagg glanced at the .45 shells littering the floor, winking in the wan light slipping around the single window shade. "And someone left you with two empty guns."

"I know enough about the law to know you ain't got no right to bust into my room." She leaned forward, blue eyes blazing, a quilt slipping halfway down her breasts. "Git out before I call the sheriff!"

Flagg turned his head. "J.C. Galen. Franco. Check the back. If you don't see him, hightail it to the livery barns. We might still be able to catch him."

When the three deputies had left, Flagg stared coolly down at the copper-haired girl, who now sat with her knees raised to her chest, holding the quilts to her neck. Her eyes were on fire, and her chest rose and fell sharply.

"I'm going to give you one more chance, Miss Saradee Jones. When did Hawk leave, and where was he heading?"

Saradee crinkled her eyes, jerked her head up, and sent spittle flying into Flagg's face. The marshal recoiled slightly, ran his gloved left hand slowly across his right cheek, and glanced at the deputies flanking him on either side.

"Hound-Dog. Bill. Press." Flagg lunged forward, ripping the two quilts from the girl's grip, laying her naked body bare. "Help me tie Miss Jones to the bedposts."

The men stared appreciatively down at Saradee snarling and writhing on the bed like a cornered lioness, clamping her raised knees together, flexing her toes, and pressing her arms to her heaving bosom.

Big Hound-Dog Tuttle glanced at Flagg. "This ain't exactly by the book, boss."

"What isn't by the book?" Flagg said. "Restraining an obviously unfriendly witness so I can ask her a few questions?"

Bill Houston said, "Titty up or titty down?"

"Down," Flagg said. "I'm thinking this girl's pa was too soft on her. She needs a good strapping across her naked ass . . . till she remembers where Hawk's headed."

"Spare the rod, spoil the child," Press Miller chuckled.

Flagg holstered his pistol and reached for one of the girl's ankles. She uncoiled like a snake and struck, bounding off her heels and flying across the bed. She tucked her knees into her chest and slammed both kneecaps into Flagg's chest.

The marshal grunted and stumbled back. The girl clawed at his eyes with both hands as she drove him to the floor.

"Goddamn!" Miller exclaimed, grabbing one of the girl's flailing arms.

Saradee screamed like a wildcat. She jerked the marshal's Remington from his holster and thumbed the hammer back. Before she could lower the barrel toward Flagg's head, Bill Houston grabbed her wrist.

Pop!

The slug thumped into the ceiling.

Houston jerked the revolver out of her hand, then smashed the butt across her left temple. Saradee grunted and flew to the floor to Flagg's left, where Hound-Dog Tuttle held her down with a knee between her pointed breasts.

She stared up, wild-eyed, breathing hard, blood glistening on her temple. In the wan light, her naked body appeared swarthy as an Indian's.

Flagg climbed to a knee, his upper lip curled, his colorless eyes set like stones. Three clawlike scratches bled on the nub of his left cheek, while his right brow was torn, the blood dripping into the corner of his eye.

Tuttle had a firm grip on both the girl's wrists, his knee still firmly planted on her chest. Saradee scrunched up her eyes and winced at the pressure, barely able to breathe. She halfheartedly kicked her naked legs.

Flagg stood and ripped the bottom sheet from the bed, stretched it out between his hands, and ripped it down the middle. "Now, where were we?"

When they had the girl tied belly down on the bare mattress, wrists and ankles secured to the four brass posts, Flagg removed his hat, coat, and cartridge belt. He unbuckled the belt holding his pants to his lean hips.

He glanced at the three deputies. "You men head on out and stuff your fingers in your ears while I . . . *interrogate* the witness."

Miller grabbed his rifle and smiled at Saradee lying spread-eagle, her slender back flaring out to her hips and round buttocks. "Sure you don't want us to stay and observe the procedure, Marshal?"

Flagg shook his head and doubled the wide leather belt, then dipped the tongue in the water bowl atop the washstand. "Search the livery barns. I'll be along just as soon as Miss Jones decides to spare her ass and cooperate."

As he grabbed his shotgun from against the wall and moved toward the door, Tuttle glanced toward the bed. Saradee lay with her face to the wall, her hair a thick, coppery mass across her shoulders. She breathed sharply but said nothing.

Tuttle grabbed the doorknob. Flagg raised the wet belt and slammed it down hard across the girl's bottom.

Crack!

The girl tensed. She stopped breathing for a second. Then she sucked a deep breath, and her back resumed rising and falling sharply. A red, rectangular welt stretched across her buttocks.

"Now, then," Flagg said as Tuttle followed Houston and Miller into the hall and closed the door behind him. "Need I continue, Miss Jones?"

The three deputies paused before the room's closed door. They looked at one another expectantly, saying nothing, holding their weapons slack in their hands.

Crack!

The men jumped slightly.

Houston grinned. "Damn, that's gotta smart!"

Tuttle said, "The book they gave me when they swore me in and gave me the badge didn't say nothin' about interrogatin' prisoners this way."

"That's because you weren't after a man like Gideon Hawk." Miller slapped Tuttle's shoulder with the back of his left hand, and started toward the stairs. "Come on, let's check out those livery barns."

Crack!

Tuttle flinched and headed after his partners.

He was halfway down the stairs, the desk clerk standing with one hand on the newel post, staring warily up at him, when the sound of the belt smacking bare flesh again rose like the report of a small-caliber pistol.

The oldster hitched his glasses up his nose. "What in blue blazes is goin' on up there?"

"Nothin' that concerns you," Houston told him. "Go on and get yourself some breakfast."

Halfway across the lobby, Tuttle blinked when the belt lashed across the girl's bottom. Harder than before. Upstairs, she gave a sharp grunt through clenched teeth but didn't mutter a word.

Later, all six deputies were waiting with their horses at the west edge of town, when Flagg strode toward them. The sun was nearly up, a salmon wash in the sky behind him. Flagg moved stiffly, mouth set in a grim line.

"Get anything out of the her?" Houston asked.

Flagg shook his head. "Strangest damn girl I ever laid eyes on."

"Maybe she didn't know," Tuttle said.

"She knew, all right." Flagg plucked a stogie from his shirt pocket and scowled back in the direction of the hotel. "Tighter-lipped than most men I've interrogated . . . though I left my mark on her hide."

"Doesn't matter, boss," said Franco Villard. He threw the reins of Flagg's steeldust to him. "We found the livery barn he stabled his horse at. Fresh prints indicate his horse has one new shoe, built up a little on the left." He canted his head to indicate a fresh hoof print on the dew-damp trail before them.

Flagg flushed eagerly and grabbed his saddle horn. "Well, what we waiting for?"

Flagg tipped his hat low and spurred the steeldust into a westward gallop. Falling in behind him. Press Miller turned to Villard. "Isn't it 'What *are* we waiting for?' "

Wending his way through the Arizona desert, Hawk headed back to his current hideout in the Anvil Mountains near the Mexican border.

Three days south of Cartridge Springs, he put the grulla down a rocky ridge crest until he was no longer outlined against the sky, and stopped. He hooked a leg over his saddle horn and dug into his shirt pocket for his makings sack.

Rolling the smoke, he peered into the broad, rocky canyon before him, an ancient Mexican village strewn about the slopes, with a shallow, glistening river threading the canyon's bottom.

Home sweet home.

Hawk let his eyes range along the canyon and both ridges, habitually scouting trouble. The adobe and stone hovels wedged against both slopes were nearly indistinguishable from the boulders and tough clumps of brown and iron-gray brush.

The smoke wafting up from several chimneys smelled of burning piñon and mesquite, roasting goat meat and chili peppers.

Sangre de la San Pedro, the village had once been called. Blood of St. Peter. Gringo prospectors had renamed it Bedlam, and the name had stuck even amongst its Mexican inhabitants, only a handful of whom remained after the silver veins had pinched out.

Hawk touched fire to the cigarette, drew the smoke deep into his lungs.

It was good to be back to the secluded little canyon.

Since Tombstone had begun booming to the east, few risked the Apache-infested trails to come here. Hawk, however, had found an hacienda on the northern ridge—abandoned since its inhabitants had been wiped out by a fever several years back. Several months ago, he'd taken up residence there, to rest between manhunting expeditions up north.

It was more room than he needed, but most of the locals avoided the place, as they believed it haunted by the lost souls of those who'd died there writhing and screaming in fevered agony. His bedroom balcony offered a good view of the village below the ridge as well as both ends of the canyon. Few came or left without Hawk knowing about it.

The breeze pushed against his face.

If he were smart, he'd stay here. Settle down. Give up the hunt. The hacienda was certainly big enough to raise a family, and there were enough acres for a kitchen garden and horses.

Hawk took another deep drag off the cigarette, then stripped it, letting the tobacco drift away in the breeze. He tipped his hat brim low against the westering sun, slipped his right boot into the stirrup, and heeled the grulla forward, letting it pick its own way along the switchbacking trail.

The village gradually pushed in around him, the mostly abandoned hovels crumbling back to the iron-red caliche from which sage, cactus, and wild berry shrubs grew. He passed the dusty fountain that saw water only when it rained. Circling the main square, he continued out of town, past a low, pink adobe hut around which a half dozen goats chewed the short brown grass and a one-eared cat sunned itself atop a pile of neatly stacked pine and cedar logs in a saffron ray of sunlight slanting down from the western ridge.

"Gideon!"

Beyond the goats, Hawk stopped the horse.

In the river down the grade to his left, fifty yards away, a young woman knelt in the water that rippled white over shallow rocks. She was a slender girl with long black hair. Naked, her tan skin glistening wet in the late light, she waved. Her full breasts were pear-shaped, heavy against her chest. Hawk saw the white line of her teeth as she smiled.

Feeling the throb of desire, Hawk waved back.

"Are you home for good this time?" she called in broken English. Juliana Velasquez had been born here in the village, to a Mexican mother and a gringo prospector father, both taken by the fever.

Hawk raised both arms and shoulders. "For a time!" What did "for good" mean, anyway? Until he got the urge to go sniffing out outlaws north of the border, to go hunting again . . .

A stream of broken Spanish rose sharply, and Hawk saw that the old woman who'd raised Juliana, Dona Carmelita, was kneeling on the shore, her back to Hawk. The old woman was surrounded by clothes and bedding stretched out amongst the shrubs and boulders. Her Spanish was too fast for Hawk to follow. She gestured angrily at Juliana.

The girl's shoulders shook with laughter as she covered her breasts with one arm and turned away. But she kept her head turned toward Hawk, smiling. With her free arm, she waved, lifting her hand high above her head.

Hawk returned the wave and gigged the grulla along the trail.

Soon he was threading his way up the northern ridge, along the boulder-strewn trail switchbacks. He turned the last bend through a stand of pecan trees and entered the shaded, dusty yard, the old hacienda standing behind a four-foot adobe wall—a sprawling, two-story structure with shuttered windows and narrow, stone stairs rising to a heavy oak door. Sunlight glistened on the whitewashed walls and red-tiled roofs, faded and crumbling from age and neglect.

On a second-story balcony on the house's left end, a

man's head appeared suddenly. Just as suddenly, it was gone.

Hawk stopped the grulla, his heart thudding.

Smoke came to his nostrils, flavored with burning pine and roasting javelina. Someone had moved into the hacienda.

The head appeared again, a bearded face beneath a steeple-crowned sombrero. As a rifle barrel swung toward Hawk, he threw himself out of the saddle. The rifle's barrel stabbed smoke and flames, the sharp report sounding like a cannon blast in the early evening silence.

6.

JUST IN TIME FOR DINNER

THE slug spanged off a rock as Hawk hit the ground and rolled. The horse reared, whinnied, and lurched into a gallop, racing across the yard.

"You're just in time for dinner, gringo!" A guttural laugh rose from the balcony. "Have some hot lead! A little tough, but it really stays with you!"

Three quick rifle cracks. The slugs slammed into the ground where Hawk had first hit. Now he lunged to his feet and ran, crouching, toward a boulder.

Another laugh, another rifle shot.

Another man shouted in Spanish, "What wonderful luck, Jesus! A *norteamericano* to assist with our target practice!"

A rifle boomed twice, both slugs cracking into the boulder as Hawk leapt behind it. Grabbing a revolver in each hand, he edged a look around the boulder's right side.

Powder smoke wafted in an open window behind a dead orange tree. A ruddy, unshaven face appeared in the window. Sunlight flashed off the rifle as the man raised the butt to his shoulder.

The maw flashed and the report echoed around the yard as the slug slammed into the boulder, spraying shards.

When Hawk lifted his head again, the man in the window was smiling, teeth glistening in the sun's rays angling through the orange tree.

Two other men crouched behind the wall of the dining room balcony to the left of the window. One of the men fired his two pistols resting atop the balcony wall. Hawk ducked as one slug blew up gravel to his right and the other barked into the rock with a deafening spang.

Keeping his head behind the boulder, Hawk lifted his chin and cupped his hands around his mouth. "You fellas are in my house!"

Another pistol shot. "Oh? We thought it was abandoned, senor."

"You thought wrong, amigo. You got five minutes to pull out!"

"Pull out?" The shout rose from the window. "But we like it here!" The man chuckled. The rifle boomed, barking off the rock, pelting the brush behind Hawk with shards.

Hawk thumbed both pistol hammers back. His trigger-happy boarders were no doubt on the run from *rurales* on the other side of the border. Border toughs. Nasty as the rats Hawk had had to run off when he'd first moved in.

He lifted his head and snaked the Russian over the top of the boulder, aimed at the man in the window who was aiming his rifle at Hawk. Hawk's Russian spoke a half second before the man's rifle boomed.

The rifle bullet tore up a sage clump two feet before the boulder. Peering through his own gun smoke, Hawk saw the man in the window stumble back and turn slightly, blood beneath his left eye glistening in the sunlight.

Hawk ducked behind the boulder as the two men in the balcony cut loose with pistol fire, shouting Spanish epithets.

When the barrage faded, Hawk set both his pistol barrels on the boulder and fired, blowing a sombrero off a head and tearing adobe from the lip of the balcony wall.

Large chunks of mortar flew in all directions. He emptied the Colt, holstered it, and, not waiting for the two men in the balcony to reload, bolted off his heels and ran toward the hacienda.

When he was ten feet from the low wall encircling it, a hatless, black-haired head bobbed up from behind the balcony wall. A revolver flashed and popped, the slug plunking into the dirt a foot to the left of Hawk. Hawk dove behind the wall, extended the Russian over the top, aimed, and fired.

The shooter grabbed his right shoulder and screamed. Falling, he triggered a stray round into an empty planter.

Hawk straightened, leapt the four-foot wall, and ran toward the hacienda. A pistol on the balcony barked twice. Both shots spanged off the crumbling flagstones behind Hawk's pounding heels. Running up the steps, Hawk returned the two shots. As the gunmen ducked down behind their barricade, he gained the top of the entrance steps and stopped.

He holstered the Russian, sprang off his feet, and grabbed a viga pole protruding from the sun-faded adobe. He swung up and over the balcony wall. One of the ambushers cursed and raised his revolver toward Hawk. Hawk kicked the man's wrist. As the gun flew from the man's hand, Hawk dropped to the balcony floor.

The ambusher—a burly Mexican with curly salt-and-pepper hair—reached across his thick waist for the bowie knife sheathed on his left hip. Hawk straightened, met the challenging gaze of the big man before him, the extended knife flashing in the westering sunlight. The wounded man lay on the floor, reaching for a .36 Colt Navy two feet to his left.

Hawk feinted right. The big Mexican slashed with the knife.

Hawk bolted straight back, caught the man's arm on the backswing, and rammed his right fist into the man's soft belly. The man grunted. Hawk slammed his fist into the man's jaw, the solid smack followed instantly by the crack of breaking bone. Dropping the bowie, the stout Mexican stumbled straight back, overturning a wicker chair and falling with a shrill Spanish curse.

The other Mexican grabbed the Colt. Cursing, he swung it toward Hawk, but before he could thumb the hammer back, Hawk drew his Russian and fired. The slug painted a round, red hole on the man's neck, just below his bulging Adam's apple, knocking him back against the balcony wall.

Hawk turned the Russian toward the big man, who had his right hand on a Remington sheathed in a silver-trimmed shoulder holster. His eyes darted to Hawk's revolver. His hand froze on the Remy's butt. He smiled tensely as he removed his grasp from the Remy and opened both his hands.

"Enough," he said in Spanish. "Perhaps we can share the quarters, uh, gringo?"

Hawk shook his head and curled his upper lip. "Something tells me you snore."

The man's eyes flicked to the Russian. He blinked, shifted his anxious gaze again to Hawk's eyes, lines stretching across his forehead. He opened his mouth to speak. Hawk's Russian spoke instead, carving a neat, round hole through the man's forehead, silencing him forever.

The Russian smoking in his right hand, Hawk looked around. Silence except for the breeze sliding down the mountain behind the hacienda, whispering in the pine tops. Keeping his ears pricked for other bushwhackers, Hawk reloaded the Colt and the Russian, then dropped the Colt back into its holster.

Extending the Russian in his right hand, he turned and walked into the hacienda. Because the local Mexicans believed the house haunted, it had pretty much been left as the family who'd lived here had left it after the smallpox had felled them one after another. He moved through the dining room and sitting room—both immaculately furnished, though layered in dust and spiderwebs and littered with rodent droppings—past the foyer in which the rifle-man from the window lay dead on the flagstones. He came to an inner courtyard lit with wan evening light, a green sky showing above the walls webbed with corded, brown vines.

Above Hawk's head, the ceiling creaked slightly.

He studied the heavy timbers, listening. Another creak sounded, as if a foot had been lightly planted on the floor.

Hawk turned to a recessed door across the hall, and tripped the latch. He opened the door slowly, climbed seven steps, and stood looking over a large room with a large canopied bed and four scrolled posters. A balcony with a wrought-iron railing opened on the room's left side, facing south. One of the balcony's heavy wooden doors was closed; the other stood half open.

The room was appointed with several deep rugs—one of sleek black panther skin—several heavy wooden chairs, a bureau, and an armoire that filled an entire wall. An elk trophy with an enormous rack hung over the bed. On the other walls and in niches were book-lined shelves, carved tables, paintings, and tapestries.

The room had probably been the sleeping quarters of the casa's hacendado. It afforded a good view of the village and the trail leading up the mountain from the valley. Hawk had slept in the room when he'd holed up here before taking up the scout once more. He intended to hole up here again.

Apparently, someone else had found the room hospitable in his absence.

The air was rife with cigar smoke. The bed and one pillow held the indentation of a body, as if someone had been resting there only moments ago. On the bedside table stood a brandy bottle and a half-filled glass. Several cigar butts lay in a silver-lined ashtray. One sent a thin stream of smoke curling along the blue lamp looming over it.

Flexing his fingers on the Russian's grips, Hawk moved around the end of the bed, heading for the balcony. He glanced to his right. On the floor beside the bed stood a

pair of calfskin saddlebags, the flaps dyed red, fancy
stitching trimming both pouches. Hawk continued toward
the balcony, moving slowly, setting each boot down quietly
on the fieldstone flags.

He was four feet from the half-open door, holding the
revolver straight out from his chest, when the door burst toward him, knocking the Russian aside. A short man bolted
out from behind it—a middle-aged hombre with a black
silk tunic, red sash, black patch over his right eye, and thin
gray hair combed straight back from a low forehead. The
man held a short-barreled pistol in his right fist.

The old bandito snarled as his pistol popped.

Hawk's Russian spoke once, twice, three times, the bullets punching through the man's chest and belly. The old
jackal—probably the group's leader—gave a defiant cry,
his face creased with pain as he stumbled back against the
balcony rail. With another scream, he fell backward over
the rail, twisting and dropping out of sight. His body made
a soggy, crunching sound as it hit the stone patio below.

Hawk stepped forward and winced. Pain seared his left
side. He looked down. The bullet had torn through the side
of his sheepskin vest. He opened the vest. A small blood
splotch grew on his shirt, about six inches below his left
armpit.

"Shit."

He pressed his right hand over the wound, winced at the
burn. Probably the bullet had carved a nasty furrow between his ribs, maybe kissing a bone or two. He'd heard it
ricochet off a bedpost behind him.

Ignoring the burn and the blood dribbling down his
side, Hawk checked the rest of the house for more bushwhackers. Twenty minutes later, he deemed the house
clear, though nearly every room was littered with the bandits' food scraps and cigar butts. He found a dusty brandy
decanter in the hacendado's office, apparently overlooked
by the bandits, and took several slugs, quelling the pain
from the bullet burn.

Stuffing his neckerchief under his shirt, he got the blood

to clot, then hauled the dead bandits one by one out of the hacienda to a deep ravine at the east end of the yard.

He rolled the last man into the gorge and took a breather, pressing his neckerchief once more to the wound, then headed back toward the hacienda.

On the way, he spied his grulla cropping bunch grass in a cedar grove. He led the mount to the stable flanking the hacienda and saw that he'd acquired a cream Arab and three mustangs, all snorting and contentedly munching hay inside. When he'd finished tending to the grulla, adding water to the stock troughs, Hawk draped his saddlebags over his left shoulder, hefted his Henry rifle in his right hand, and walked outside.

Barring the stable doors, he turned and started toward the house. Nausea and fatigue flooded over him like warm, black water. He sank to one knee, dropping the rifle and saddlebags.

He cursed, then froze as the sound of galloping hooves rose on the other side of the yard. He peered into the shadows as a horse and rider crested the hill and angled toward the hacienda. Wincing and clutching his side, feeling the blood ooze from the burn, he reached for his rifle.

The hoof thuds faded, and the horse snorted. There was the squeak of saddle leather. "Gideon!"

It was Juliana Velasquez.

"Vamos!" she ordered the horse.

He looked up as the girl galloped the pinto toward him and then dismounted as the horse skidded to a stop ten feet away.

She dropped to one knee beside him. "Are you all right? I heard shooting!"

Up close, Hawk hardly recognized her. Normally, she wore long gray skirts that old Carmelita sewed from flour sacks along with loose blouses and rope sandals. Her hair usually tumbled carelessly about her narrow shoulders.

Tonight, she wore a purple satin blouse cut low in front and a slitted black skirt that fit her tight as a drumhead across her hips and thighs. A black ribbon served as a choker, and her slender feet were clad in flat-soled black shoes.

"Coyotes moved in." Hawk pulled his hand away from his side. The palm was covered in red. "They were kind enough to throw me a welcome home party."

Juliana sucked a sharp breath and closed her fingers around his arm. "We must get you inside."

"Was just headin' that way."

"I will help," she said, taking his arm as he picked up his rifle and saddlebags and then stepped off the walk and angled toward the hacienda's rear door.

She walked so close to him that her left breast nudged his arm, and he found himself looking down past her buffeting black hair to the blouse, the matronly breasts jostling inside, pushing at the fine, purple satin.

She looked up at him, her features flushed with excitement. "Where are they now? Did they flee?"

"Dead."

Her expression changed to curiosity. Then they were entering the hacienda and making their way through the musty, sepulchral shadows, heading toward the kitchen and the fire and the succulent smell of roasting javelina.

She pulled out a chair at the dining room's long, oak table. He sat down heavily, grabbed her wrist, let his gaze wander across her alluring outfit once more. His eyes moved to her face. "Go back to the village. I can't be sure there aren't more banditos heading this way."

"I am not afraid." She turned away, grabbed a pan, and began working a pump handle. Her gaze flicked across his chest and shoulders. She wasn't yet eighteen, but her eyes flashed with womanly interest. "Take your shirt off, and I will tend your wound."

7.

JULIANA VELASQUEZ

YOU'RE a defiant she-male, Juliana Velasquez."
She looked at him and smiled.

When Hawk had found a whiskey bottle and a glass, he removed his shirt and sat back in his chair. While he rolled a quirley from his makings sack, the girl wrung out a cloth in the pan, sat down beside him, and began dabbing the wound with the cloth.

The kitchen was lit by only the dying fire beneath the javelina, the meat hissing and dribbling grease onto the coals with a smoky sputter. The girl's hands worked gently. Hawk could smell her rose water perfume.

"I didn't know you had left," she said as she wrung the cloth out in the pan, casting him a sidelong glance before dabbing again at the wound. "I rode up to go fishing, and you were gone. And then . . . a month later . . . you return."

Hawk splashed whiskey into the glass and winced as the cloth caught at his torn flesh. "I had business up north."

Truth was, after two months here in the hacienda, enjoying the mountain quiet, he'd gotten antsy and had ridden north to check the Wanted posters in Cartridge Springs. There he'd learned that the freight office and bank had been hit, a young mother and her son left to die on the boardwalk.

No point in informing Juliana of such grisly business, however. She knew nothing of him besides his name and that he used to be a lawman. That was enough. It was best for her that way. Best for him. He probably wouldn't be here long.

He thought he'd take to the peace and quiet, and maybe even decide to stay here forever. But hunting the Shadow Nielsen bunch had whet his appetite for the hunt, and Bedlam was too quiet, too far off the killing trail.

"You should tell me when you go," the girl gently chided. She looked at him crossly, then rose, dropped the cloth in the pan, and disappeared into a pantry. She reappeared a moment later, holding a long white tablecloth out before her, and ripped it in half. "Will you be leaving again?"

Tossing one half of the cloth onto the table, she folded the other lengthwise and sat down beside him. He sipped the whiskey and looked at her, his agate-green eyes standing out against his Indian-dark face. "I'm not the one, Juliana. Not the one for you."

She ripped a swatch from the long cloth, balled it up, poured whiskey over it, then touched it to his side. Hawk jumped at the liquid burn, nearly dropping his cigarette. She glanced up at him, a devilish light in her eyes. Holding the whiskey-drenched cloth over the wound, she drew the longer cloth around his waist.

"Do not think I have to go—how do you say?—*soliciting* for a man's attentions. I have had many young men try to spark me. There is one now, a rich prospector's son. He comes down from Vernal Peak once each month for supplies, says he wants to take me to San Francisco in California." She tied the cloth around Hawk's waist, not looking at her hands, but staring into his eyes, the corners of her mouth turned up slightly. "A very handsome man, big shoulders, broader even than yours."

Hawk snorted. "Broader than mine. Well, then, that's the boy you wanna hogtie."

Her brows furrowed slightly with annoyance. "I cannot help it if you are too soft in the head to know a good woman when you see one. If you are more interested in going north and doing God knows what . . ."

Hawk drew deep on the quirley. She was fishing again, trying to find out who and what he really was. She had some vague idea that he was a pistolero, or an outlaw who rustled or robbed or both, staying one step ahead of the law.

Let her entertain her romantic fantasies. Aside from satisfying his natural male cravings, he had no time for women—even a young woman as beautiful as Juliana Velasquez, who'd dressed so alluringly this evening.

As she knotted the cloth around his waist, jerking it taut with more vigor than necessary, she glanced up at him seductively. "Tonight, I would like to stay here . . . with you . . ."

Hawk took her wrists in his hands. "If you get your heart broke, Juliana, it'll be your own fault."

She dropped her eyes thoughtfully.

After a time, she nodded. She lifted her eyes again to his. Pulling one of her hands from his grasp, she reached up and touched her fingers to his broad, angular face. She rose up slowly, moving her head toward his, parting her lips.

He leaned toward her and closed his mouth over hers. Her lips were soft and ripe, her tongue shyly probing. After a time, she pulled away, lowered her hands to his naked shoulders, stout as wheel hubs, and ran them slowly down his bulging, powerful arms, gently prodding the tough skin with her fingertips.

"If my heart is broke, the fault is mine." Her brown eyes flashed whimsically. "If *your* heart is broken, the fault is *yours*."

Hawk laughed. He grabbed her shoulders, kissed her, stood, picked her up, and slung her over his shoulder like a feed sack. She gave a startled cry and laughed, wrapping her arms around him.

"Gideon!"

"We're off to the ogre's chambers, princess!"

"Oh!" She clutched him tighter. "Your side!"

"You wrapped it so damn tight, one of my lungs is closed!"

Laughing like a drunken lord, Hawk grabbed his rifle in his free hand, then walked out of the kitchen and through the sitting room, running into furniture. The sun had set, and the hacienda's cluttered, high-ceilinged rooms were dark as caves.

In the large bedroom at the top of the seven steps, he tossed the girl onto the bed. She bounced and laughed, breathing hard, the leather springs sighing. Hawk could barely see her; the room was dark as pitch.

"Damn," Hawk said. "Matches. I'll be right back."

"Don't leave me—it's dark!"

"Sit tight, princess. The ogre will return."

He returned to the kitchen, grabbed a whiskey bottle and his saddlebags off a chair back, then, as an afterthought, took a long fork and speared a haunch of the roasted javelina onto a clay platter. His stomach grumbling as the fragrant steam rose to his nostrils, he stumbled back to the bedroom. He threw his saddlebags over a chair, set the meat on a table, and lit a lamp, casting the room in dim light and dancing shadows.

He turned to the bed, and his breath caught in his throat.

Juliana lay naked there upon the multicolored quilt, propped on one elbow, her delicate shoulders awash in her raven hair. Her almond legs were curled, one slender foot resting atop the other, her toes flexing slowly. Her full, brown breasts slanted toward the quilt, the pebbled nipples jutting. Her brown eyes glittered seductively in the lamplight.

Hawk frowned. "You've done this before."

"Only once," Juliana laughed. "And it was awful!"

"What makes you think this will be any better?"

"Carmelita."

Hawk had kicked out of his boots and was unbuckling his cartridge belt. He froze and jerked his head toward her, shocked. *"Carmelita?"*

Juliana stretched her long legs out, then brought her knees back to her chest. "She said if I didn't seduce you, she'd give it a shot herself!"

"So much for pious old Catholics." Hawk unbuckled the cartridge belt and slung it over the same chair on which he'd hung his saddlebags. He slid the chair to within a few feet of the bed, then unbuckled his pants.

Juliana looked at the two large revolvers jutting from their holsters. "Billy the Kid—that's who you are!"

"Close." Hawk peeled off his long underwear bottoms and kicked them under a table, then turned to the bed. Juliana's eyes dropped to his jutting member. They stayed on it as he climbed onto the bed and knelt beside her.

"You sure about this?"

She shuttled her gaze from his member to his eyes, and back again, then cupped his balls in her hand. Her voice was high and thin, barely audible. *"Por favor?"*

As the night deepened and lobos called in the hills, a cool breeze pushing through the cracks in the balcony doors, Hawk fed pine and cedar logs to the fired clay-and-brick hearth. He and Juliana ate in bed, smearing their bodies in grease from the meat, and making love over and over again.

After one such bout, the girl lying belly down beneath him, a pillow under her thighs, Hawk pulled away and dropped his legs to the floor. Juliana arched her back and sighed, breathing hard, her skin glistening with sweat and grease.

She turned her head toward him. "Where are you going?"

"Hot in here." As he moved toward the balcony doors, his right elbow knocked his cartridge belt and saddlebags off the chair. A long, blond braid and a carved wooden horse tumbled out of one flap, along with a dented coffee cup, a tobacco sack, and a box of .44 shells.

Juliana propped her head on an elbow as Hawk picked up the cartridge belt and draped it over the chair. "What are those?"

He glanced at her. She was gazing down at the braid and the wooden horse.

Hawk picked up the braid—a lock of his wife's hair, which he'd clipped after cutting her down from the cottonwood tree in their backyard, before the ladies from their church had prepared Linda's body for burial. The wooden horse—a black, rearing stallion—was the last piece his young son, Jubal, had carved before Three-Fingers Ned Meade had hanged the boy above Wolf Creek, west of their hometown of Crossroads, Nebraska Territory.

Holding the braid in one hand, Hawk scooped the horse off the floor with the other. He ran a thumb over each, then slid both back into the pouch. "Keepsakes."

When he'd stuffed the other possibles back under the flap, he returned the bags to the chair, keeping the pistols angled toward the bed, and walked naked to the balcony. He threw open the doors, standing in the cool breeze that pushed against him and tousled his dark-brown hair. Turning, he added another small log to the fire, then climbed back into bed, crossing his arms behind his head and staring up at the beamed ceiling.

She scuttled up beside him, placed a hand on his chest, and gazed into his face. "Have I convinced you to stay?"

He ran his hand through her hair, caressed her smooth cheek with his thumb. He held her gaze but said nothing.

Her forehead creased with perplexity. "What is it you are searching for?"

"Peace." Hawk lay his head back and returned his gaze to the ceiling. "A place in this world where my wife and children won't be killed by madmen."

In the berserk state that had overtaken him in the wake of his family's demise, the irony of trying to find, or create, such a peace with his six-guns was lost on Gideon Hawk.

Juliana stared at him for a time, then glanced at the saddlebags hanging over the chair. Her own gaze darkening as she saw that he was lost to her now, glowering off into space, she gave a shudder.

She drew her body close to his, absorbing his warmth. She wrapped an arm around his waist, rested her cheek upon his chest, and closed her eyes.

8.

AMBUSCADE IN CHARLEY'S WASH

FLAGG and the six deputies lost Hawk's trail in a torrential desert rain squall, then picked it up again the next day. At noon, the sun burning through their hats and sucking the moisture from their bodies so that their eyes felt like glass marbles in dry, bony sockets, they let their horses draw water at a runoff spring. Stretching their legs, the men filled their canteens and built cigarettes.

Flagg walked the top of a low knoll and stood beside an ancient, gnarled saguaro. He plucked his makings sack and surveyed the trail ahead—an old trace deep-gnawed by iron-shod ore wagons—through a maze of strewn boulders, broken sandstone pillars, and narrow, twisting ravines rising to blue mountains.

Standing with the other men near the horses, Bill Houston studied Flagg's back. Finally, taking a long drag from his cigarette, he strode up the knoll and stood beside Flagg.

The tall, gray-haired, hard-eyed marshal stood staring into the high mountains looming darkly against the western sky.

Houston took another puff from his quirley. Blowing

smoke, he said, "Tell me somethin' straight up, will you, Marshal?"

"Haven't I always been straight with you, Bill?"

"Why do you hate Hawk so much? He was a good lawman at one time. Understandable how he went nuts after his family was killed and a crooked prosecutor sprang the killer." Houston mopped his brow with a blue handkerchief. "I ain't defendin' the man, you understand. He must be stopped. I'm just wondering why you *hate* him so bad."

Flagg cut a slit-eyed glance at the tall, angular Texan. "What makes you think I hate him so bad, Bill?"

"The way you flush up every time his name's mentioned." Houston paused, held Flagg's cold gaze. "The harsh . . . measures . . . you've taken to find the man."

Flagg turned away, slipped his own cigarette between his thin lips. "He's a lawman turned outlaw. Nothing worse in my book, Bill. Every time he deals his own justice, he's making a travesty of the U.S. Constitution—a travesty of my job and my beliefs." Flagg rose stiffly on the balls of his feet and exhaled a deep breath, smoke streaming from his nostrils. "I'd say a vigilante of his caliber warranted a few harsh *measures*, wouldn't you, Bill?"

Houston stared at him. He smiled woodenly, nodded, then walked back down to where the others stood with the horses. Flagg remained atop the knoll, smoking. Annoyance plucked at him, a parasite squirming deep in his loins.

He hadn't told Houston the truth.

He hated Hawk, all right. But not only for the reasons he'd given the Texas lawman. Several months ago, Flagg had watched Hawk do away with a gang of killers south of the Mexican border. Flagg had had Hawk in his rifle sights, and he hadn't killed him, out of sympathy.

Since then, the rogue lawman had eluded Flagg for nearly a year. And because he hunted and killed known criminals with no regard for any law but his own, he was cheered on by the public. In many towns Flagg had visited while stalking Hawk, he'd come upon local lawmen and express agents who'd refused to post Wanted dodgers bearing Hawk's likeness.

In making a travesty of the bona fide law of the land, Gideon Hawk had become a damned hero.

And bona fide lawmen like D.W. Flagg had become laughingstocks.

Flagg took the last drag off his cigarette and stared at the high, blue mountains. His fury burned anew. He dropped the butt, mashed it out with his boot toe, and walked back down the knoll.

He cupped his hands around his mouth. "Mount up!"

That afternoon the lawmen were climbing out of a shallow canyon between two stark, sunburnt ranges when they heard guns popping to the south.

Flagg halted his steeldust, sat staring in the direction of the shots, one eye slitted.

"What the hell you s'pose that is?" said Franco Villard, sitting his own horse to Flagg's right.

"That's Charley's Wash yonder. When I was deputy sheriff of Tucson, mule trains were always getting ambushed in there."

Flagg paused, frustrated. He looked ahead along the trail, ran a gloved hand across his mouth, cursed. "We'd better check it out."

By the time Flagg reached the base of the ridge, the shooting was growing intermittent, the sporadic shots spanging off rocks and drowning the muffled pleas of wounded men.

As the deputies caught up to him, Flagg swung down from the saddle. He slid his Winchester from the boot, angrily rammed a shell into the breech, and started up the ridge. "Watch your heads. I need every man for Hawk!"

He jerked sideways to avoid a coiled rattler, leapt over a clump of Mormon tea, and spurred himself into a jog.

The shots grew even more sporadic, as if the fight on the other side of the ridge were winding down.

Press Miller squinted against the sun glare. "Mescins, you think, Marshal?"

Flagg was breathing hard, watching where he planted his boots. "No doubt. They kill each other for farting upwind around here."

"Damn," Garth said. "I'd like to shoot a Mexican, take his ears home to a whore I know." He hurried to add, "But only if they're breakin' the law, of course."

Flagg cocked an eyebrow at him.

"She hates Mexicans," Garth explained. "One gave her a vicious knife scar a few years back in Abilene. Keeps askin' me if I shot any Mescins. She wants to wear the ears around her neck."

"If you're gonna bring Mex ears to a whore," asked Miller through a grin, leaping a barrel cactus, "what're you gonna bring your wife?"

A shrill cry rose from the other side of the ridge. *"No!"*

The seven lawmen stopped, raised their rifles, and peered toward the ridge top.

"Please, don't . . . don't shoot me!"

The last word hadn't died on the man's lips before a pistol spoke twice. From this distance the shots sounded like snapping matchsticks.

Flagg hurried up the ridge, muttering, "Spread out and stay low. I want to know what the hell's going on before we show ourselves."

As the others fanned out toward the rocks to his right and left, Flagg doffed his hat and knelt behind a split boulder, peering through the rock's V-shaped notch. Charley's Wash—a deep, rocky, brushy cut—lay on the other side of the ridge, choked with boulders washed down by an ancient river.

At the bottom of the wash, the bodies of a handful of soldiers lay sprawled across the rocks, their dark-blue uniforms torn and bloodstained. A dozen men in dusty trail garb milled about the bodies, tearing rings from fingers and peering into mouths for gold fillings. The gunfire had died, but the smoke still ebbed along the arroyo's floor.

One of the bandits held a pair of saddlebags over one shoulder, the large U.S. markings on both flaps flashing in the sunlight as the bandit stooped to pick up a Springfield trapdoor carbine.

A low whistle sounded on Flagg's left.

Flagg turned. Galen Allidore stared at him, bushy red brows furrowed. "Army payroll?"

Flagg nodded. The soldiers, probably out of Fort Huauchuca, had no doubt been hauling payroll coins to a remote outpost when the bandits had attacked.

Shouting erupted below, and Flagg returned his attention to the wash. A blue shirt slid through the brush—a soldier making for a nest of rocks and saguaros to the marshal's right. Behind the man, several bandits yelled and pointed. One raised a rifle, and fired.

The blue shirt dropped behind a paloverde, then reappeared as the soldier continued forward on his hands and knees. Above the incessant whine of cicadas, Flagg heard the man's sharp grunts and anxious pleas.

The bandit who'd fired the rifle, and two others, descended on him quickly. The man with the rifle kicked him flat. He clamped his boot down on the soldier's back as he spoke to the other two bandits, one of whom threw his head back and laughed.

The bandit raised the rifle to his shoulder, aiming at the soldier's head.

Bunching his lips, Flagg snapped his own Winchester up. He aimed quickly and squeezed the trigger.

A half second after the bark, the hard case with the rifle jerked his head up. His rifle came up, as well, the pop reaching Flagg's ears a full second after the barrel puffed smoke. Dirt and gravel sprayed two feet from the wounded soldier's head.

The other two bandits snapped their own heads to the man with the rifle, who stumbled forward, tripping over the wounded soldier and dropping to his knees.

"Open up on the sons of bitches!" Flagg barked.

He ejected the spent cartridge, rammed a fresh round

into the breech, then slid the barrel to one of the two other men near the soldier.

As the man faced Flagg, crouching and spreading his feet and grabbing the six-shooter from the holster on his right hip, Flagg sent him tumbling into the brush, the wounded outlaw inadvertently triggering his revolver into the head of his dead cohort.

Around Flagg, the deputies' rifles sent a crackling fusillade into the wash. Like Flagg, all six were expert marksmen, and in that first volley a half dozen bandits were sent sprawling into the chaparral around the soldiers they'd ambushed.

Several others returned fire, shouting and arguing, then turned and ran. The man with the payroll money leapt a rock as he scrambled south along the wash.

Flagg had run halfway down the ridge, snapping shots with his carbine. Now he stopped, aimed at the retreating back of the man with the loot, and planted the rifle's sights on the fancy stitching adorning his bullhide vest, between his shoulder blades.

He fired as the outlaw dodged behind a saguaro. The shot plunked into the cactus, spraying dust and cactus bark. Continuing down the wash, the man edged a look behind, then disappeared over a rise. Several of the deputies' shots kicked up caliche and snapped mesquite branches as the last of the outlaws disappeared over the rise and was gone.

Flagg continued down the rise, thumbing cartridges from his belt and feeding them into his Winchester's loading gate. He glanced at Press Miller. "You and Hound-Dog fetch the horses."

Hound-Dog glanced at him. "What about Hawk?"

"Hawk can wait. I know where he's heading. We're going after those bushwhacking sons of bitches!"

Flagg repressed a smile. Not only would he bring Hawk to justice, he'd secure the Army payroll. He'd have his name in all the papers. A candidate for the territorial governor's office couldn't ask for better publicity.

Shit, he'd be a hero.

"These bushwhackers need to be taught a lesson," Flagg said, lowering his rifle toward an outlaw writhing in the brush at the base of a saguaro. "And I'm just the teacher."

The outlaw, bleeding profusely from two holes in his chest, looked up at Flagg, his gray-green eyes pinched with pain. One-handed, Flagg pressed his carbine's barrel against the man's sweat-glistening forehead.

The wounded man's jaw tightened, and his eyes flashed horrifically.

Villard, kicking over a dead outlaw to Flagg's right, glanced at the man before Flagg, and frowned. "Hold on, Marshal."

"Deputy Villard, this man appears to be reaching for a pistol—wouldn't you agree?"

Villard looked at the man. The outlaw stared back at him, his eyes beseeching. He couldn't be much over seventeen, with jug ears, hollow jaws, and close-cropped, sun-bleached hair. His hands were nowhere near a gun. In fact, both his holsters were empty.

Villard's eyes returned to Flagg. "We playin' by Hawk's rules, now, Marshal?"

Flagg pressed his rifle barrel hard against the kid's head. "Trying to keep this man alive, when he is obviously mortally wounded, would be a waste of our time. Time better spent hunting that travesty of justice, Gideon Hawk." Flagg's pinched eyes flicked toward Villard. "Wouldn't you agree, Deputy?"

Villard didn't say anything for a moment. He glanced at Houston and Allidore, who'd both stopped their survey of the wash to regard Flagg incredulously. Villard looked again at the wounded man, bleeding out in the rocks and cactus.

Slowly, the deputy nodded his head. "Appears that way to me, Marshal."

Flagg squeezed the Winchester's trigger. The outlaw's head exploded. The young man slumped onto his right shoulder, kicking his legs and clenching his fists, as if furious at having been killed.

"We got two more over here," Bill Houston called to Flagg, nodding at two men writhing on the ground between him and Allidore.

"They're both going for weapons," Flagg said. "Kill them."

Houston glanced at Allidore, shrugged a shoulder, then shot his man in the head. Allidore's rifle spoke two seconds later, drilling a rangy half-breed in a red bandanna through the heart.

Houston and Allidore glanced at each other and chuckled.

Flagg heard screeching and looked up. Already, the shaggy black crosses of buzzards winged in lazy circles over the draw. He turned away from the man he'd shot and walked around the wash, inspecting the other bodies.

The eight soldiers were dead. Flagg found one more living outlaw, the man's back rising and falling faintly as he lay facedown in a cactus patch. He'd been shot in the side and through one leg.

Flagg shot him in the back of the head.

A horse whinnied, and Flagg turned to see Miller and Hound-Dog Tuttle riding their own mounts down the ridge, trailing the outlaws. As they approached the bottom of the wash, Flagg reached for his reins.

"What about the soldiers?" asked Bill Houston.

"We'll bury them later," Flagg said, swinging into the leather. "*After* we've retrieved the payroll money."

He turned the steeldust in the same direction the other bushwhackers had fled, and gave him the spurs.

Behind him, climbing clumsily into his own saddle, big Hound-Dog Tuttle glanced at Villard. "Think this'll put him in the governor's office, Franco?"

"If it don't get him—and us—killed." Villard kneed his grulla into a trot.

"That's 'doesn't,' " Press Miller corrected. "*Doesn't* get us killed."

The others laughed and galloped after Flagg.

•   •   •

Flagg and the deputies ran their horses hard, following the bushwhackers' trail—six shod horses splitting wind for the border. Flagg wouldn't let them make it. He'd be damned if they'd make it.

When they'd ridden for an hour, Flagg could tell from the tracks that the outlaws' horses were tiring. On a ridge, the lawmen spied a long dust trail stretching out across the flat, chaparral-tufted desert below. The falling sun colored the dust orange, the six horses at the head of it, dun brown.

The lawmen heeled their mounts down the ridge.

"They know we're back here," Flagg said. "A couple keep slowing up and turning their horses to look back."

"Beware a bushwhack," said Press Miller. "They're good at it."

"I'm good at sniffing out a bushwhack, too," bragged Flagg.

He was. That's why, following the trail between two low, piñon-studded scarps, he halted his steeldust as he stared down the horse's left shoulder.

"What is it?" asked Allidore, following Flagg's gaze.

"There were six horses a moment ago. Now there're only five."

A rifle barked angrily. Hound-Dog Tuttle's hat flew off his head.

As the shot echoed shrilly around the scarp, Flagg shucked his Winchester and, turning the horse with one hand while jacking a fresh shell with the other, snapped the rifle to his shoulder.

Smoke puffed around a thumb of rock jutting out from the scarp's base. There was the metallic rasp of a rifle being levered, then flames stabbed through the smoke as the shooter fired again.

Flagg cut loose with his carbine, sending lead through the smoke, peppering the scarp. The slugs barked off the rock, whining.

A man screamed, stumbled out from behind the boulder. He dropped his rifle, lost his hat, and danced around, enraged and disoriented. Flagg's bullets, ricocheting off the scarp, had shredded the man like shotgun pellets.

Hound-Dog and Villard both sent more .44 rounds through him, laying him out flat on his back, twitching.

Flagg turned his horse down trail. "Let's go!"

They galloped down a hill. Ahead lay a ravine, a purple gash in the fading light. At the lip of the ravine, sunlight shimmered off a rifle barrel.

"Ambush!" Flagg shouted.

A half second later, a rifle snapped. The slug twanged off a rock to Flagg's left, caused a horse to whinny behind him.

As more shots roared and smoke puffed amidst the brush along the lip of the cut, Flagg turned his mount in a full circle, dodging lead. "Three of you follow me! Three head right! We're gonna get behind 'em and send some blue whistlers up their assholes!"

Flagg turned his horse left, toward the bushwhackers' far left flank. Houston, Miller, and Villard galloped behind him, hunkered low in their saddles, dusters flapping like wings. The other three lawmen raced right, returning fire, their silhouetted figures disappearing behind a billowing veil of gun smoke.

Flagg felt a bullet curl the air behind his neck as his horse plunged into the ravine. The horse's front hooves hit the gravel and tough, brown brush at the bottom, nearly sending Flagg over its head. He grabbed the horn and gave an involuntary grunt as the air whooshed out of his lungs.

Sucking a breath and raising his Winchester, he gigged the horse westward along the draw. After three lunging strides, he saw the shooters lying along the ravine's northern ridge. Three of the five turned toward Flagg, while the other two, hearing the other lawmen driving in from the west, jerked looks in that direction.

"Goddamnit!" one shouted. It was the man who'd carried the Army payroll bags—a stocky gent in a black vest, with a broad pitted face framed by black muttonchop whiskers.

Flagg jerked back on the reins with his left hand. With his right, he aimed the Winchester, snapped off a shot. The steeldust wasn't stopped, and the jostling nudged the slug into the bank beside the outlaw's right elbow.

The man cursed again and fired at Flagg. A quarter second later, Press Miller's rifle drilled the man through his chin, knocking him back against the bank. He had an amazed look on his face as he clutched his jaw with one hand while holding his rifle with the other.

The other deputies cut into the outlaws, Tuttle's barn blaster roaring amidst the rifle cracks.

Hearing slugs whistling around him, plunking into the ground before and behind him, Flagg triggered his Winchester, levered, and triggered again. His steeldust was well trained, but not even a well-trained mount would keep its hooves planted amidst this much gunfire.

Still, at least as many slugs found targets as flew wild.

Less than a minute after the deputies had stormed into the ravine, all the outlaws lay stretched out along the bank, dead.

The rotten-egg smell of cordite filled the ravine. The smoke hung like fog. Blood spurted from a dead outlaw's neck, making a wet sound like water squirting from a high-pressure spring.

While the deputies sat their horses, staring sullenly at the dead men flung every which way upon the bank, Flagg gigged the steeldust forward. The horse climbed the bank and stopped beside the dark-haired hard case.

Leaning out from his saddle, Flagg scooped up the saddlebags with his rifle barrel and draped them across his bedroll.

He rode back down to the bottom of the wash, waved powder smoke away from his face, and turned back to regard the corpses.

"We made short work of these bastards," said Tuttle,

chuckling and reloading his shotgun. "Hawk should be a turkey shoot."

Flagg looked at him. "You think so, do you?"

Tuttle shrugged.

Flagg laughed, reined his horse around, and rode off down the wash.

9.

SECRET PLACE

SITTING under pines along the needle-strewn creek bank, Gideon Hawk watched the cartridge casing bob along a riffle in the gently flowing stream.

Hawk had filled the casing with paraffin to help it float upright, and drilled a hole through it. After stringing fishing line through the holes and attaching the line's other end to the homemade pole he'd crudely fashioned from a willow branch, he'd skewered a cricket to the hook.

Flashing in the sunlight angling through the pines, the cartridge bobbed between two mossy stones, nudged a yellow cottonwood leaf, and dropped into a placid hole on the other side of the stream.

The cartridge jerked suddenly into a small cavern made by an old pine root overhanging the river, and disappeared beneath the dark water.

Somewhere in the depths of Hawk's memory, a phantom called. "Pa, I think I got one!"

Jubal Hawk stood on the far side of Wolf Creek, not far from their house in Crossroads, Nebraska Territory, the boy's cane pole bent out over the rushing water. Six-year-old Jubal—stocky and dark-haired with eyes the same blue as his mother's—ran along the creek while staring hang-jawed at the droplet-beaded line angling into a deep hole on the downstream side of a beaver dam.

Hawk laughed. "Give your pole a tug straight up, and pull him in!"

The boy gave the pole a tug and stretched a happy, terrified grin at his father fishing on the opposite side of the stream. "The hook's set, but it's really big. It's a hog! *Gotta* be!"

Hawk propped his own pole against the log he was sitting on, then rose and leapt onto the beaver dam. As he threw his arms out for balance, he made his way to the far side of the stream. The water, still icy this early in the spring, slid across his boots, riffling against his trouser cuffs.

Jubal exclaimed with boyish glee as he tugged on the pole and backed away from the water, a suspender falling off a shoulder. One foot slipped in a patch of star moss, and he fell on his backside, his floppy-brimmed hat tumbling off his head. "Dang!"

"Hold on to the pole, Jubal!"

The pole had slipped out of the boy's hands, but now as Hawk leapt from the beaver dam and onto the boy's side of the stream, Jubal grabbed the pole and pushed up on his knees.

"It's gonna break," he cried, lifting the pole's end and peering into the stream.

"It's all right," Hawk said, staring into the water along the bank, choking back a laugh. "Give it another tug and you've got him."

Hawk stepped back, wet boots squishing, as Jubal planted a hand on one knee and pushed himself to his feet with a grunt. When the pudgy boy got his other foot under him, he took a deep breath, balling his flushed cheeks, and tugged on the pole hard with both hands.

There was a light, frantic splash as the fish shot out of the water and landed on the bank.

"Oh, boy!" Jubal ran over to where the huge fish lay on a cottonwood root.

Only, the fish wasn't as huge as it had first appeared shooting out of the stream. In fact, it wasn't much of a fish at all—just a little half-pound bullhead swaddled in moss, spruce-green watercress, and a soggy tree branch.

The boy looked down at it, crestfallen. He kicked the tree root. "Darn! I thought it was a lunker!"

Hawk laughed and tousled the boy's hair. When he'd unhooked the gasping fish and returned it to the stream, he leapt onto the beaver dam, throwing his arms out for balance. "Back to work, son. Nothin' comes easy, you know!"

"But Pa, I really wanted it to be a lunker to show Ma!"

The boy's voice was drowned out by another. Someone was squeezing Hawk's arm and calling his name. Hawk turned his head to find Juliana staring at him, her brown eyes showing concern, both hands wrapped around his forearm.

She knelt beside him, her bare legs and feet curled beneath her, her soft, white skirt pulled up above her knees. Her hair hung in flowing waves across her shoulders, framing her tan, heart-shaped face.

She glanced at the stream, the bridge of her nose deeplined with excitement as she sprang up and down on her thighs. "Gideon, you've got one! You caught a fish! Pull it up!"

Hawk turned to the stream. But instead of the teabrown, sun-dappled water churning over the rocks, what he saw was a large cottonwood tree standing atop a steep hill. The tree was silhouetted against a stormy sky, its branches thrashed by pounding rain.

Thunder rumbled. Lightning stabbed witches' fingers across the gauzy darkness.

Hanging from a stout branch of the tree was a pudgy young boy, turning this way and that in the wind . . .

"Jubal . . ." Hawk muttered.

His heart tumbled in his chest. He choked back a sob, squeezed his eyes closed, and gave his head a hard shake.

When he opened his eyes again, the tree was gone. The stream appeared before him, the alpine air smelling like pines, mushrooms, and damp soil. Sun-dappled water churned over the rocks, washing a branch into a small trough and sweeping it downstream.

Hawk felt a wetness on his cheeks. His throat was still tight.

He glanced again at Juliana. She stared into his face, her own features flushed with worry. She squeezed his forearm and caressed his cheek with her other hand, thumbing away a tear—a soft, sweet caress.

Her voice was barely audible above the stream. "Are you all right, Gideon?"

For a half second, Jubal's hanging corpse flashed again before his eyes. He blinked, and it was gone. There was only Juliana beside him, smelling like rose hips, the wind blowing her hair and buffeting her low-cut blouse. Before him was the stream in the deep, pine-studded canyon north of the hacienda . . . and the mesquite pole in his hands, jerking ever so slightly as a fish fought at the other end of the line.

On the other side of the river, where the cartridge had sunk, water rippled, splashed by a small, silver tail.

Hawk stood and raised the pole above the stream. The fish rose from the water and tail-danced across the surface as Hawk swung it toward him and grabbed it out of the air.

He turned a smile toward Juliana. "A brooky. Just like the ones I used to catch with my—" He cut himself off, stared at the slippery body writhing in his hand.

Standing beside him, Juliana regarded him soberly. "Your son?"

Hawk removed the fish from the hook, dropped it in a wicker basket lined with mint.

"And the braid that fell out of the saddlebag last night. That belonged to your wife."

Hunkered down beside the basket, Hawk turned to her. "How? . . ."

"I overheard men talking in the cantina while you were gone. You are the vigilante lawman from the north."

Hawk dropped his gaze. He hadn't thought anyone in the village had heard of him, much less recognized him. News traveled fast, even to the remotest places on the frontier, it seemed. Traveling, he often used the alias George Hollis. He hadn't thought he'd have had to use it here.

"They said your son was murdered. Hanged. And your wife hanged herself out of grief."

"From a tree in our backyard." Hawk looked at her. "Why didn't you tell me you knew?"

"I was waiting for you to tell me." She stared at him for a time, the sunlight glittering in her eyes. Then she dropped down beside him, threw her arms around his neck. "Gideon, I am sorry! You can find peace here . . . with me. You can forget!"

Hawk wiped the fish slime from his hand, pulled her toward him. He held her tightly for a while, savoring the warmth of her supple body against his, brushing away spruce needles that had caught in her hair as they'd led a burro down the southern ridge.

"Come on," he said pushing her away and kissing her cheek. "We're gonna need more fish than that for lunch. I don't know about you, but I'm hungry."

He rose and baited his hook with another cricket and tossed the line into the stream. She watched him for a time, eyes dark and pensive, then stood, retrieved her own pole, and tossed the line into the creek.

Behind her, the burro chewed leaves from a willow branch. The crunching sound mingled with the stream's rush and the forlorn cry of a hawk circling high above the crenellated canyon walls.

Later, as Hawk dropped his third small brook trout into the wicker basket, he turned to Juliana. She sat along the stream, her back against a boulder, the pole in her hands, long, tan legs stretched toward the water. Her face was tipped up to the sun.

"I'll fetch wood for a fire."

She glanced at him over her shoulder, eyes brightening. "No, wait. I know a better place for a picnic." She rose and retrieved her line, then slid her pole under a strap on the burro's back. When she'd untied the animal, she began leading him upstream, beckoning to Hawk as she made her way barefoot along the rock slabs sloping toward the creek.

"Come. I will show you a secret place!" She walked a few more steps, then turned another glance toward him, her eyes bright with conspiracy. "But you have to promise not to tell another soul!"

Hawk chuffed and threw the basket over his shoulder. Hitching his gun belt on his hips, he grabbed his Henry rifle and began following the girl along the canyon's stony floor. They traced a bend, forded the stream, and meandered along a side canyon cloaked in cool shadows and cut down the middle by a meandering freshet. The girl walked along the base of the canyon's right ridge—a sheer slab of andosite shooting straight up toward the sky, the wall pocked here and there with swallows' nests.

A golden eagle swooped through the canyon, so close to Hawk's left shoulder that he could see the keen, copper eyes, see the wind rippling the dun feathers, and feel the whoosh of wind as it passed.

Juliana stopped, tethered the burro to an ironwood shrub, and slung a burlap pouch around her neck. She glanced at Hawk coming up behind her, then crouched down beside an oval cleft low in the canyon wall. She met his gaze, smiled beguilingly, then dropped to her knees and scuttled into the cave.

Hawk frowned, concern stabbing him. Clefts in canyon walls were favorite haunts of mountain lions, even bears. "Hey, where you going?"

"Follow me!" Her voice was muffled by rock, and he realized the cleft must be deeper than he'd thought.

Hawk glanced at the burro. The burro regarded him dully, twitched its ears, then chewed some leaves off the ironwood bush.

Hawk adjusted the basket's strap on his shoulder, knelt down, and, leaning on his Henry's butt, peered into the cleft. It smelled stony, not as musty as he'd imagined, as if somehow it was vented from within. He couldn't see much. What he assumed was the girl's shadow shuffled back in the gauzy purple depths.

Hawk looked around, his innate wariness of enclosed places pricking the hair under his collar. Reasonably sure that he and the girl were alone in the canyon, he dropped to all fours and slid into the cavern.

He crawled under a low ceiling for ten feet before it suddenly rose and he was able to stand. The passage here was a good seven feet high.

"This way!" The girl's voice sounded sepulchral, echoing faintly off the rock walls.

Hawk peered straight into the mountain. Juliana stood sideways, peering back at him. She was silhouetted by the natural light beyond her.

As Hawk started forward, she turned and continued moving through the narrow corridor. He kept her slender figure in sight as he moved between the pitted, jutting walls, stepping over rocks and cracks, hearing his boots squishing slightly on the damp, uneven floor.

As if from far away, water trickled tinnily.

"Hurry!" Ahead, Juliana had stopped in what appeared to be a broadening of the corridor. Natural light fell down around her, glistening in her long black hair. "It's going good today!"

"What's going good?" Hawk muttered, continuing forward and running his hand along the wall, noting the flecks of fool's gold etched into the andosite, the smell of bat guano tainting the otherwise fresh, damp air pushing against his face.

His boots and spurs began echoing more loudly as he approached the opening. The sound of tumbling water grew louder, as well, the humidity rising. Juliana had drifted from sight. The soft, blue daylight before him was etched by a fine mist.

The walls on both sides pulled away as he strode into a large oval room. Thirty feet above the floor, the ceiling slanted at a forty-five-degree angle, a good half of it missing, as if a lid had been opened onto the blue desert sky.

The room's floor was strewn with the rubble that had once been the ceiling. On the room's right side, water tumbled into the opening from the mountain slope above. It splashed over the strewn rubble and flowed down into a crack it had carved deep into the floor, the black, bubbling water churning out of sight somewhere below.

Hawk didn't look at the underground river for long.

Juliana herself had captured his attention, standing as she was—glistening wet and naked—on a pile of black rocks at the base of the waterfall.

Hawk's heart quickened as he watched her turning this way and that in the tumbling water, her dark hair pasted against her head and back. Her heavy breasts jutted proudly, swaying as she moved and laughed, turning to show him her slender curving back and round, pale buttocks over which the water slid then tumbled about her feet.

She turned a complete circle, faced him again, ran her hands under her breasts, cupping them and lifting them and throwing her head back and opening her mouth to the water—a beautiful, bewitching desert sprite.

He ran his eyes from her navel to her breasts and then to her face. She stared at him, her broad smile filled with girlish charm. "This is my secret place. I found it long ago, when I was just a kid. You won't tell anyone?"

"Your secret's good with me," Hawk said, staring at her, transfixed.

"Come," she cried, "the water's fresh!"

Hawk dropped the fish, stood his rifle against the wall, and was out of his boots and clothes in less than a minute. Naked except for the bandage encircling his chest, he climbed the rubble, felt the icy mist pushing against him, then stepped into the cold stream tumbling down the wall . . . and into Juliana's outstretched arms.

The cold water did nothing to dampen his desire.

He ripped off the bandage, tossed it away, and held the girl close, kissing her deeply, running his hands up and down her wet back and buttocks. Finally, he sat on a boulder behind the falling water, drew her onto his lap, and spread her legs.

Sucking his lips and tongue into her mouth, she straddled him, pressing her firm breasts against his chest, the jutting nipples prodding him gently. She adjusted her hips and thighs, pressing her hands against his face, groaning.

And then she slid over him.

10.

END OF THE TRAIL

NEARLY twenty-four hours after coming upon the ambuscade in Charley's Wash, D.W. Flagg crested a high ridge and pulled back on his steeldust's reins.

He squinted into the canyon gaping before him, the thatch roofs and red-tile roofs of the *pueblito*'s humble dwellings shimmering in the late afternoon sun. The river winding along the south side of the village glistened like the skin of a Mojave green rattler.

The six deputies drew rein on either side of the marshal, their sweating horses blowing and nickering as their hooves, heavy from miles of continuous travel, scuffed the talcumlike trail dust and clattered on the rocks.

"Bedlam," snorted Franco Villard, reading the faded sign leaning along the trail. "What the hell kinda name is that?"

The others snorted and chuckled while Hound-Dog took a long swig from his canteen, the water dribbling into his sweat-soaked beard.

Flagg's expression remained implacable. "Not long after gold was discovered in these mountains, a crazy prospector killed his three partners with a pickax. Then he killed a padre, a couple *putas*, and a vaquero passing through town." The marshal's eyes ranged along the floor of the canyon. "Appropriate that a crazy lawman would end up here."

"Why you so sure Hawk's still here?" asked Miller. "He might have had a mouthful of whiskey in the cantina, and rode on."

"The trail ends here," Flagg said. "There's no village beyond here. The only trails are old Indian or prospector tracks. Deep canyons, real devil country, all the way to Mexico."

Scowling warily into the canyon, Hound-Dog looped his canteen over his saddle horn and rested his shotgun across his knees, his finger through the trigger guard. "How we gonna play it? There must be twenty, thirty shacks down there. He could be holed up in any one of 'em."

"We start with the bartender, and go from there." Flagg kneed his steeldust down the hill and into the canyon.

Villard chuckled and gigged his horse after Flagg. "Good idea."

The seven lawmen rode two abreast, dropping gradually between the motley collection of ancient Mexican hovels and prospectors' shacks. Only a few people, mostly old, leathery-featured Mexican men, milled about the street. As the procession passed a cracked, brush-roofed adobe, an old Mexican woman in a sacklike white dress and bright green shawl regarded them from a clothesline sagging between two spindly pepper trees. A goat near a well coping watched her closely, as if fascinated by her industry.

A low fire burned in the yard. A little boy, long black hair hanging in his eyes, poked in the fire with a stick. Glaring at the lawmen, the old woman yelled at the boy, beckoning, then, grabbing the boy's hand, ambled into her shack. She cast the lawmen one more angry glance, then closed and locked the door with an angry click of a thrown bolt.

"You think she's gonna invite us to supper?" Hound-Dog quipped to Franco Villard.

Hound-Dog stopped chuckling when he heard sharp, frenetic panting to his right. He turned to see a small, three-legged dog—mostly white but with a black snout and a black ring around its right eye—dash out from a gap between two board shacks and head for Hound-Dog's horse. When the dog closed to within four feet of Hound-Dog's chestnut, the mutt barked shrilly. The tired horse, startled by the unexpected attack, whinnied and reared. Hound-Dog, as fatigued and surprised as his horse, grabbed at the saddle horn, missed, and flew back off the horse's left hip.

Cursing shrilly, he hit the ground on his back.

As his horse sidled away, snorting indignantly at the angry cur, the dog closed its small jaws over Hound-Dog's trouser cuff. Growling like a miniature bobcat, it gave the cuff several fierce shakes before releasing it, backing up, and yipping into Hound-Dog's face, its tiny eyes pinched with spite.

"Goddamn mutt!" Hound-Dog clawed his Colt from its holster, and thumbed back the hammer. The dog seemed to know what the big deputy intended. It pivoted on its one rear heel and ran back the way it had come.

Hound-Dog aimed and fired. The bullet plunked a rain barrel as the dog dashed behind it, disappearing into the gap between the shacks.

Press Miller had grabbed the reins of Hound-Dog's skittish chestnut.

Flagg turned his own horse toward the deputy still floundering on his backside, Colt extended.

"Deputy, holster your revolver!" Flagg's jaws were clamped with fury. "Get back on your goddamn horse and try to look like a professional instead of a drunken court jester!"

Hound-Dog had lost his hat, and his sweat-streaked face was even dustier than before. Lowering the pistol, he looked up at Flagg with a wounded expression.

Behind him, Miller laughed. "Don't you know it's bad luck to shoot a three-legged cur, Tuttle?"

Ignoring the chuckles of the other men around him, Hound-Dog holstered the Colt, grabbed his hat, and heaved himself to his feet. Cursing under his breath, he climbed gingerly into the saddle, the leather creaking beneath his weight, the chestnut rolling its eyes warily.

"Keep your eyes skinned," Flagg ordered the men, glancing sharply along the street at the mostly empty windows staring back at him. "That shot *probably* announced us to Hawk." He added through gritted teeth to Hound-Dog, "You stupid bastard!"

Villard gave Hound-Dog a menacing look.

"Damn dog scared my horse!" the big deputy retorted, slapping his dusty hat against his thigh.

Flagg flared his bloodshot eyes at him. "Shut up!"

The procession continued down the street, angling toward the town's lone cantina on the street's right side—a big structure hammered together from milled lumber during the prospecting boom, and painted spruce green, with dark-blue lettering above the porch roof announcing TATE GREEN'S SALOON. On a bullet-scarred shingle hanging from two rusty chains beneath the awning, sun-faded letters boasted, "Best Wimen in the Territory!"

Two vaqueros in steeple-crowned sombreros and bright serapes stood on the porch, holding beer mugs and staring at the approaching lawmen. Both men wore looks of bemusement, but the expressions faded as Flagg drew up before the hitch rack and swung down from his saddle. As the lawman looped his reins over the rack and mounted the stoop, the eyes of both vaqueros acquired guarded, wary casts.

One removed a brown paper cigarette from his mouth as Flagg stopped before him and shuttled a bland stare between the men. The marshal reached inside his corduroy jacket to remove a quarter-folded sheet from his shirt pocket. His black-gloved, right hand shook the paper open, turned it toward the two vaqueros.

Flies buzzed around the beer glasses as the men lowered their gazes to the Wanted dodger.

"Ever see this man?" Flagg asked, waving the flies away from the beer with his left hand.

The taller of the two men lifted his eyes to Flagg. His face was so sun-seared it looked black behind a two-day growth of beard. He shook his head.

Flagg glanced at the shorter man. A fly crawled around in the man's beer-damp, salt-and-pepper beard. "No, senor."

Flagg stared into the man's eyes, glanced at the other lawmen behind him, then turned and sauntered through the batwing doors. The other lawmen, each glaring in turn at the two vaqueros, followed Flagg into the building. All but Bill Houston, that was. The tall Texas lawman paused before the two vaqueros.

"You bean eaters better be sure you never saw Hawk." Houston spit tobacco quid onto the shorter man's scuffed, high-heeled boots. "I find out otherwise, I'll fix ye so you have to take your food mashed up in tequila and drink it from a beer glass."

Houston spit a quid on the taller man's boots, then turned and pushed through the batwings.

Inside the cantina, Flagg moved slowly toward the bar in the shadows at the back of the big, wood-floored room. There was only one customer, a gray-bearded old Mexican wearing a ratty brown poncho, relaxing at a table to Flagg's left.

A lump on the left side of the poncho bespoke a pistol in a shoulder holster. When the old Mexican looked up from his beer glass, two tequila glasses on the table before him, Flagg saw the scarred cheeks and the eye patch over the right eye. The scars were two matching Xs, carved by an Arkansas toothpick across each cheekbone. The same weapon had poked out the eye.

I'll be damned, Flagg thought. Palomar Rojas. The marshal would have recognized those scars anywhere—received from the deputy sheriff Rojas had cuckolded

some twenty years ago in Fort Worth, even before Flagg
himself had once hunted the old border rough for rustling
Texas seed bulls back and forth across the Mexican border.
He'd never caught the man. Long ago, he'd heard he'd
been killed by Lipan Apaches.

If the old man recognized Flagg, he gave no indication.
He glanced at the marshal and the six deputies with keen
interest—it wasn't every day a half dozen territorial lawmen rode into Bedlam—then hunkered low in his chair and
buried his face in his beer schooner. He probably wasn't
rustling anymore, but he still had paper on him . . . as well
as a contempt for lawmen.

Flagg and the deputies continued to the bar reaching
across the back wall. The counter wasn't just pine planks
stretched across beer kegs, but an ornate mahogany affair
with an elaborate back bar complete with lamps and mirrors. Obviously, the place had been built with high hopes
for the town—hopes that the short-lived tenure of the gold
boom had dashed.

Flagg glanced at the barman standing behind the glistening wood—a burly, gray-haired, blue-eyed American
who'd been slicing a chicken on the back counter when the
lawmen had entered. He stood frozen now, cleaver in hand,
regarding the lawmen with an expression of both appre-
hension and amusement, his blue eyes glittering.

Out his dusty front windows, he'd no doubt seen the
three-legged dog's attack on Hound-Dog.

He leaned on his fists, his glance dancing from one copper badge to another. "You boys shoulda let me know you
was coming. I'd have baked a cake."

"Whiskey," Flagg said.

The barman set up seven glasses in a row on the pine
planks. He ran an unlabeled bottle over each glass, splashing whiskey into each and a good bit on the bar. He corked
the bottle, set it on the bar, and returned his gaze to Flagg
as each deputy moved up to take his glass.

Keeping an eye on Palomar Rojas as well as the door by

glancing in the mirrors behind the back bar, Flagg threw back his whiskey.

"Another?" the barman asked.

Flagg shook his head.

"It's a long, dusty trail to Bedlam," said the barman, lip curled wryly to show a chipped eyetooth. His face was big and clean-shaven, the eyes ironic. Flagg had noticed he moved with a limp. "The town's so poor the Apaches don't even bother with us anymore. Sure you wouldn't like one more drink to cut the desert?"

"Maybe just one more," Flagg said.

When the barman had slopped whiskey into each law-man's glass, Flagg dug the Wanted dodger out of his pocket and set it on the bar. He picked up his glass and turned sideways, studying the dusty street before the saloon, running his eyes along the roof lines.

If Hawk was here, he no doubt knew that Flagg was here now, too. No time for carelessness. The marshal knew from past experience that trailing Hawk was like trailing an old, wounded wolf—a wolf who'd slept too long in the moonlight.

A wounded, half-crazed wolf. One that didn't flinch at killing his old colleagues. In Colorado, he'd killed a young deputy, Luke Morgan, whom Hawk himself had not only trained but had considered a younger brother.

"Seen that man around?" Flagg said out of the left corner of his mouth. In the periphery of his vision, he watched the barman turn the dodger toward him, bow his head over it.

The man studied it for a half second, then turned the paper back toward Flagg.

"Think you must've taken a wrong turn somewhere." The barman picked up the whiskey bottle. "Next round's on the house." He splashed more whiskey into the deputies' glasses. Several had rolled cigarettes or lighted cigars. Hound-Dog stood with his back to the bar, cautiously studying the street. The man was a buffoon in some ways, but he'd acquired a reputation riding for Judge Bean

in Oklahoma. Even the curliest wolves learned quickly not
to underestimate him.

At a table near the wall, the old bandito, Palomar Rojas,
took a deep drag from a cornhusk cigarette, squinting
down at the loose cylinder as if worried about spilling his
tobacco. His old, dark face was obscured by smoke.

The barman poured whiskey into Flagg's glass. "I don't
make this stuff myself. It comes up from Mexico. It—"

Flagg grabbed his Remington from its holster and
shoved the barrel up under the barman's chin, tipping the
man's head back. The man splashed whiskey onto the bar,
over the Wanted dodger. The liquor dribbled onto the floor
around Flagg's boots.

Pressing the barrel hard against the barman's jaw, Flagg
spoke through gritted teeth. "You might want to look once
more at the likeness on that flyer. Make real good and sure
you haven't seen that man. He might be callin' himself
Hollis. George Hollis."

The barman looked down his cheeks at the whiskey-
drenched flyer. His voice was pinched with contempt.
"Maybe I did see him. Yeah. He rode through here about
two days ago. Stopped for a drink, rode on into the mountains . . ."

He looked at Flagg, his gaze flat, almost challenging.
His eyes slitted, and the corners of his mouth rose scorn-
fully. "In fact, I think he did say his name was Hollis. Yeah,
Hollis. Chiricahuas prob'ly killed him out in those badlands west of town, poor bastard."

Flagg stared into the man's sharp, insolent eyes. He set
his thumb on the Remy's hammer, had to will himself not
to pull it back and squeeze the trigger.

What did he expect from this backwater shit hole? Most
of the town probably had paper on them. That's why they
were here. They'd sooner help the kill-crazy Apaches than
any badge toters.

Flagg glanced into the mirror behind the barman's
bulky frame. The old bandito, Palomar Rojas, was gone.
His cigarette stub curled smoke up from a shot glass.

Flagg lowered the Remington and glanced at the other lawmen, regarding him expectantly.

"Have another round, boys. Relax." He holstered the pistol and strode toward the door. "I'm gonna stretch my legs."

11

"WHAT'S YOUR NAME,
MY PRETTY?"

FLAGG pushed through the batwings and stepped onto the saloon's front stoop.

The vaqueros were gone, as were the two mixed-blood Arabian horses that had been tied to the hitch rack when Flagg and the deputies had arrived. Flagg repressed a snort. It would probably be a long time before the chili-chomping waddies returned to Bedlam, after watching seven lawmen ride into town.

Both Mexicans had had "long looper" written all over their sunburnt features and brush-torn clothes. They probably hazed beef back and forth across the border in small herds that, at the end of the year, added up to droves.

Flagg looked up the street to his left, then to his right.

Just beyond the fountain standing sentinel over the town's shabby main square, a stocky gent in a low-crowned sombrero was riding out of town on either a big horse or a mule—it was hard to tell which from this distance. Flagg could tell from the slumped shoulders and the old hat, however, that the rider was Palomar Rojas.

As the man's retreating back was hidden by the dry, concrete fountain between him and Flagg, the marshal stepped into the street, again bringing Rojas's slouched figure into view until the old bandito's mount rose to the crest of a rocky rise then disappeared down the other side.

Flagg scratched his dusty beard, then slipped his steel-dust's reins from the hitch rack and swung into the saddle. He turned the horse into the street. Door hinges creaked behind him.

Hand slapping his Remington's grips, he turned to see a girl standing in the doorway of a small general merchandise shop sitting kitty-corner to the saloon. A pretty, brown-eyed girl with thick black hair piled atop her head. She wore a white dress with a red sash around her waist, and a low-crowned straw sombrero, the leather thong sagging beneath her chin. She'd been laughing, her sparkling eyes and dimpled cheeks accenting the heart-wrenching beauty. But when she'd seen Flagg, her eyes flicking to the badge on his vest, the laughter began fading from her face, a cloud scudding over the sun.

Inside the shop, a woman was speaking ebulliently in Spanish. A face appeared over the girl's right shoulder— the broad, flat face of a much older Mexican woman wearing a long green apron, a pencil stuck behind her left ear. When the woman's eyes met Flagg's, she fell silent, glowering, placing one hand on the girl's shoulder. The woman's lips moved, but Flagg couldn't hear what she said.

Flagg smiled, dropping his gaze over the girl's large-breasted figure, down to the bare legs and feet, smooth and brown. Comely Mexican lass. Odd, finding such beauty in a place like this. A single rose in a dung-splotched desert.

It was said that Hawk had an eye for beauty. If so, he'd certainly had a look at this girl. Maybe he'd done more than just look.

Something to keep in mind.

The marshal pinched his hat brim and spurred the steel-dust westward, turning left around the fountain.

On the other side of the fountain, he glanced back. The girl had moved out from the shop and was angling northeast across the street, her head turned to regard the six sweaty, dusty horses tied to the hitch rack fronting the saloon.

Flagg turned forward and heeled the steeldust into a trot.

When the town's shacks had receded behind him, the trail narrowed to a single, rock-strewn track twisting amidst boulders and brown desert scrub. To his left was the river and an old smelter and stamping mill. The buildings' plank siding shone warped and sun-blistered against the stark, brown hills rising on the other side of the stream.

Flagg halted the steeldust and looked around for Rojas.

A din rose on his right. He turned to see a flock of blackbirds, winged shadows against the copper-colored mountainside, fly up from a large, lightning-split pine. A wide wagon trail was cut into the side of the mountain, switchbacking through cedars at a forty-five-degree angle. A rider moved out from behind the lightning-split pine.

Rojas on a dirty cream mule.

Probably heading back to his mountain hideaway. Flagg and the other lawmen had probably given him a good scare.

The marshal let his eyes range along the side of the mountain looming above the village, his gaze shuttling back and forth along the ridge. After a time, he raised his hand to shield his eyes from the early evening glare.

About halfway up the mountain, nestled amidst pines and boulders, a red-tiled roof shone brightly. Flagg stared, squinting.

Beneath the red smudge of the tiles, bulky white walls appeared. It looked like a toy house from this distance, but a house just the same. The switchbacking trail led into the yard.

Flagg stared at the house and the trail, his gray brows

wrinkled. A grand house for such an old, used-up reprobate like Palomar Rojas.

Curious despite himself, Flagg gigged the steeldust forward, then turned off the path and onto the road angling up the mountain. He'd climbed for fifteen minutes when he came to a sharp horseshoe curve overlooking a shallow canyon and offering a view of the house perched on a wide, sparsely forested shelf on the ravine's other side, about two hundred feet above the curve.

Flagg hid his horse in boulders several yards down the trail. He grabbed his field glasses from his saddlebags, then scrambled onto a rocky scarp rising over the canyon, sheathed in cedars and Spanish bayonet. Crouched low atop the scarp and concealed by the brush, Flagg doffed his hat, raised the glasses, and adjusted the focus.

The hacienda swam into view, framed by ponderosa pines and pepper and almond trees, and wedged back against the mountainside like one of those rock dwellings Flagg had seen, built by ancient Indians. This place was elaborate, but its cracked adobe walls and the general forlorn look of the place bespoke the time since a more prosperous era.

Still, a good hideout. High ground with plenty of cover, easily defended.

Flagg waited fifteen minutes before a shadow flicked through the trees to the left of the hacienda. Rojas and his cream mule rode into the yard before the low adobe wall surrounding the house. The Mexican sat his saddle, holding his hands in the air. Flagg couldn't tell—he was too far away, and Rojas faced the house—but he thought the man's head was bobbing, his jaws moving.

Finally, a shutter in one of the upper-story windows opened. A man hiked a leg up on the ledge. A big, well-put-together hombre. Even from a half mile away, Flagg could make out the square jaw and handsome features, the thick, dark-brown hair swept back from a widow's peak.

Hawk sat there casually, leg stretched out before him, resting a rifle across his thigh. He wasn't wearing a shirt.

His broad chest was encircled by a bandage, the white cloth standing out against the dark skin.

Flagg's heart hammered and his hands shook so that the glasses bobbed, obscuring the image. Finally, Hawk flicked a hand out, waving dismissively, then dropped his leg from the window ledge, retreated inside, and closed the shutter over the casing.

As Rojas turned the mule and started back the way he'd come, Flagg lowered the glasses. His heart fluttered in his chest. Sweat glistened on his pale forehead.

He swallowed a dry knot in his throat.

He scuttled back from the scarp, stood, and scrambled back to his horse, turning it onto the trail and heading back down the mountain.

Ten minutes later, he galloped past the dry stone fountain. The deputies had heard him coming, and had gathered on the saloon's front stoop, holding beer mugs and shot glasses.

Flagg halted the steeldust before them, his dust catching up to him, the deputies squinting against it.

"Round up everyone in town," Flagg ordered. "I want every soul left in Bedlam right here in front of the saloon in fifteen minutes!"

The deputies looked at each other skeptically.

"Move!" Flagg barked, leaning out from his saddle, jutting his red face toward the deputies.

They jerked into motion, setting their drinks on the boardwalk and then striding swiftly into the street, casting wary glances at Flagg as they split up and headed toward the private dwellings in the brush and boulders behind the shops.

When they'd gone, Flagg dismounted, tied his horse to the hitch rack, adjusted his gun belt on his hips, and strode through the batwings. He stopped two feet inside the room, resting his hands on the doors.

The beefy bartender stood behind the bar, both fists on the polished counter. From beneath his shaggy brows he regarded Flagg. Flagg stared back at him, his mustache up-turned in an icy smile.

The lawman sauntered across the room and placed his gloved hands on the bar top. "You lied to me, Mr. . . ."

"Baskin. Leo Baskin."

"You lied to me, Mr. Baskin."

Baskin pursed his lips, hiked a shoulder. "Why not leave him alone? I mean, the man does the job of a whole army, and he doesn't waste time with . . ." The man's sentence trailed off as he looked around for the right words.

"Justice?" Flagg said.

"The men he kills don't deserve justice."

When Flagg just stared at him with eyes like flint, Baskin added, "Come on—you boys are just piss-burned 'cause he's a better lawman."

Flagg's right hand shot up, grabbed the crown of the barman's head, and slammed his face down on the bar top.

It made a soggy smack and snap.

Wailing savagely, the barman lifted his head. His crushed nose sprayed blood, painting his apron. While his left hand grabbed the nose, impeding the blood flow, his right hand pulled a Navy Colt from under the bar. As he raised the pistol at Flagg, Flagg grabbed the gun with his right hand, jerked it from the yowling barman's grip, and smashed it against the side of the barman's head, laying open his ear.

"Fuck . . . goddamn . . . asshole!"

Clutching his nose with one hand, his ear with the other, the barman stumbled back, cursing loudly and dropping to his knees. Flagg grabbed a whiskey bottle and a clean glass, then turned and strode over to a table near the window.

He set the bottle and the glass on the table, kicked out a chair, sat down, and splashed whiskey into his glass. He lifted the glass to his lips, froze, and stared at the hand holding the glass. It shook.

Flagg scowled, threw back the whiskey, poured another

drink, dug a half-smoked cheroot from his vest pocket, and fired it.

He'd finished the cheroot and had thrown back three more shots when angry Spanish voices rose from the street. Out the dusty window before the saloon, a small crowd had gathered.

Boots pounded on the boardwalk, and the batwings squawked. Bill Houston poked his head into the saloon, turned toward Flagg while chewing a cold cigarette. "The town council is now in session, Marshal."

Flagg threw back another half shot of whiskey, and rose. He adjusted the tilt of his hat, the position of his cartridge belt on his lean hips, then headed for the door.

In the dusty street, less than a dozen Mexicans had gathered. They were talking in angry, hushed voices while the deputies stood around looking officious and holding their rifles across their chests.

The group was mostly old Mexican women in sackcloth dresses and rope sandals. A small boy buried his head in a middle-aged woman's skirt. Three old men in straw sombreros and serapes stood to one side, one smoking a corncob pipe and holding a small puppy in his arms, the puppy chewing at his gnarled, tobacco-stained fingers.

The girl Flagg had seen earlier stood with a full-hipped, black-haired old crone, who wore a bloodstained, feather-spattered apron. The crone's hands were bloody and tufted with chicken feathers. Her milky black eyes blazed at Flagg, her right shoulder shielding the pretty, full-bosomed girl.

Dipping his fingers into his vest pockets, Flagg strode into the street. He stopped before the group, cast his implacable stare across the frightened faces.

He let time stretch. "Anyone here speak English?"

No one said anything.

Flagg stepped over to the old man holding the dog. He patted the pup's head, smiling. He pinched the dog's right ear. It yipped and shook its head, tiny ears flapping. The old man slid his hand over the dog's head protectively and stepped back, glaring at Flagg over his pipe.

The marshal looked around the group of sullen, brown-eyed faces regarding him with fear and anger. His gaze stopped on the girl. He walked to her. The old woman grabbed the girl's arm and regarded Flagg with pursed lips, her eyes blazing even more than before.

Ignoring the crone, Flagg stared hard at the girl. She let her eyes flicker across his badge before dropping her gaze to the street.

With two fingers of his right hand, Flagg lifted her chin until the lustrous brown eyes met his. The eyes crinkled slightly at the corners with defiance.

"What's your name, my pretty?"

12.

PALOMAR ROJAS

WHEN the girl merely stared up at him sharply, silently, Flagg squeezed her chin between his thumb and index finger. Too many *norteamericanos* had once lived in Bedlam for her not to have picked up some English. His lips quivered inside his beard as he spoke through gritted teeth, his voice low with menace.

"I asked you a question."

The girl's eyes darkened, the lids lowering slightly. She hesitated, then, just above a whisper, "Juliana Velasquez."

Flagg eased his grip on her chin and smiled with self-satisfaction. Behind him rose the clomp of shod hooves. He turned to see Palomar Rojas riding slowly around the fountain. The old bandito sat the saddle stiffly, head tilted to one side, staring apprehensively at the small crowd gathered in the street before the saloon.

Flagg turned back to Juliana Velasquez, smiled his dull smile, released her chin, and took two steps back away from her. He turned to Rojas, who'd halted his mule in the street about twenty yards beyond the saloon, regarding the gringo lawmen darkly. He ran a gnarled, brown finger absently across his mustache, as if reconsidering how badly he needed another drink.

"Ah, Senor Rojas," Flagg said. "You've arrived just in time!"

Rojas said nothing. His dirty cream mule shook its head, dust puffing from its mane.

Again dipping his hands into his vest pockets, Flagg strode slowly toward the one-eyed bandito, who watched him darkly, occasionally casting a skeptical glance at the other lawmen and the other Mexicans forming a loose group in the street.

Flagg stopped just ahead and to the left of Rojas's mule. "I was just about to inform the good citizens of Bedlam what would happen if I caught them fraternizing with a criminal."

Rojas stared at Flagg, his lips bunched tightly, shoulders slumped beneath his serape. His scarred, bearded face was shaded by his broad-brimmed sombrero, its crown decorated with a dried hawk's foot.

The old bandito placed his right hand on his chest and said in Spanish, "Are you talking to me, senor?"

Flagg chuckled and glanced at the other lawmen standing sentinel over the crowd, rifles in their hands.

"Who else would he be talkin' to?" said Press Miller, standing with his legs spread wide near the horses tied to the hitch rack.

The bandito looked at Flagg. "I am Frederico Alvarez, senor. It is a case of mistaken identity, I think." He flicked a hand to the villagers still standing tensely before the saloon. "What do you seek with the good people of Bedlam, senor? As you can see, they are all old or very young . . ."

"We seek the man you just visited, you old reprobate. The man you alerted to our presence here." Flagg walked toward Rojas, one hand on his Remington's grip. "Now, climb down out of that saddle and take your lickin' like a man."

When Flagg was two steps from Rojas, the old bandit jerked to life. He lifted his serape with one hand while the other grabbed the old, .36-caliber Colt from the shoulder holster hanging beneath his left armpit. He'd no more than gotten his finger through the trigger guard, however, before Flagg reached up and closed his left hand over the gun. He gave it a savage wrench.

Rojas yowled a Spanish epithet and tumbled down over his right stirrup, Flagg twisting the pistol free of his hand a quarter second before the bandito hit the ground.

"Bastardo!" Rojas cried, his prunelike face etched with pain, dust puffing around him.

Flagg swung a boot up, slamming the toe under the old man's chin and throwing him straight back in the dirt. Rojas grunted as his head hit the street.

He snarled and writhed like a trapped animal. Blood trickling out one corner of his mouth, he lifted his head and rose onto his elbow, slitting his lone eye at Flagg.

"All right, lawman. Okay, uh? You have finally caught up to me after all these years." His lips spread, the sneer showing his bloody teeth. "Pin a medal on your chest."

Flagg tossed away the man's pistol and stared down at him, his chest rising and falling sharply, his face like granite. "Get up."

Breathing hard, the old bandito got his legs under him. His sombrero hanging down his back, blood dribbling down his gray-bristled chin, he stood with a wince, then assumed a fighter's stance before Flagg. The black patch covered only part of his empty eye socket.

Rojas balled his bony, brown, liver-spotted fists, anger glinting in his washed-out eye. He stepped sideways, and there was a little of the young *charro* in the old man's bearing.

Flagg stepped toward him and swung his right fist. Just before the fist could connect with the bandito's jaw, Rojas ducked. Flagg's fist whistled in the air over the old man's head.

As Flagg recovered from the wild punch, Rojas rammed his right fist into Flagg's belly. Flagg grunted. He grunted again as the old bandito landed a left in the same place.

The jabs had little power behind them, but surprise glittered in Flagg's flinty eyes. Rojas stepped back, grinning as he shifted his weight from one foot to the other, and adjusted his eye patch. Behind him, the villagers watched with wary fascination, a couple of the old men looking amused, hopeful.

Flagg returned his gaze to Rojas feinting around before him. The marshal raised his fists higher, moved his left foot forward, swung his right fist at Rojas's face. As the old bandito feinted, Flagg pulled back his right fist and jabbed with his left.

The old bandito's slow feint had moved his chin into the path of Flagg's jab. The fist connected soundly with Rojas's right cheekbone. The bandito jerked back, nearly falling, throwing his arms out for balance, his eye flickering shock.

Behind him, the other old Mexicans winced, as if they themselves had taken the blow.

Flagg smiled, stepped forward again, his right fist connecting with Rojas's jaw. The old man gave an indignant curse as he twisted around and fell on his chest. Wasting little time, his eyes pinched with anger, Flagg bent down and pulled the old man up with both hands.

"You're not finished yet, Palomar," Flagg muttered. "I've waited a long time for this."

When Rojas had his feet under him, Flagg hit him again with his right fist. As Rojas's head snapped sideways, Flagg hit him with his left.

The old man fell straight back, arms thrown out to both sides.

Flagg moved toward him, stood over him as the cursing bandito turned onto his belly, then shoved up on his hands and knees. Rojas looked up at Flagg, his cheeks and lips torn and bloody. Breathing hard, his hair curling over his forehead and nose, he grinned.

Flagg glanced at Bill Houston standing to the right of the villagers, one elbow propped on a hay cart, his rifle resting on a shoulder as he watched the spectacle with sheepish fascination.

All the other lawmen, except Hound-Dog Tuttle, had turned away and were watching the villagers, rifles extended.

"Bill," Flagg said, "would you say this man is resisting arrest?"

Houston hiked a shoulder. "'Pears that way to me, Marshal. Wouldn't you agree, Hound-Dog?"

Hound-Dog stared at the old bandito wheezing in the street, and shook his head sadly. "Some just don't listen to reason."

Flagg swung his right foot back, then brought it forward, planting the toe in Rojas's flat belly.

"Uhh!" the Mexican cried as he flew back in the street.

Several of the horses at the hitch rack turned to see what the commotion was about. Press Miller and Hound-Dog Tuttle chuckled.

Flagg stepped toward Rojas, who lay belly down in the street, his back rising and falling sharply.

"Please, stop!"

Flagg looked toward the villagers gathered twenty yards away. The girl had moved out in front of the old crone with the bloody apron. The crone had grabbed her arm and was castigating her loudly in Spanish. The girl stared at Flagg, her eyes bright with beseeching.

The puppy yipped and squirmed in the hands of the old villager with the corncob pipe. The dog suddenly broke free of the old man's grip. It leapt to the ground, ran across the street, and disappeared through a gap between two abandoned shops.

The corners of Flagg's mouth turned up, and his deep-set eyes softened with satisfaction.

He bunched his lips, swung his right boot back, and rammed it forward, burying the toe in the old man's rib cage. The air burst from Rojas's lungs with a loud, "Huh-ah!"

When he'd rolled completely over, sighing and gurgling, Flagg kicked him again, then two more times, hearing the ribs snap.

"B-bastardo . . ." The old man wheezed, blood frothing from his lips.

Finally, the marshal picked him up, steadied him with one hand gripping his serape. Rojas hung like a scarecrow before him, head lolling on his shoulders.

"What's that, Rojas? You say you haven't had enough?"

Eyes glistening with savage fury, Flagg glanced at the villagers. Several of the women had turned away. The young boy cried with his face buried in his mother's skirt. The old men looked grim. The girl stared as before, eyes etched with horror and pleading.

Flagg returned his gaze to Rojas and, bunching his lips, drove a savage haymaker against the old man's left cheek with a solid smack.

Flagg released the old man's poncho. Rojas's knees buckled. He sagged to the street and fell backward, his legs curling beneath him. He lay still, eyelid fluttering, breath whistling through his shattered teeth.

His chest rising and falling, Flagg stared down at the broken bandito. Finally, he walked over to the girl. She stared at Rojas, her eyes shiny with tears.

"You tell the others that if they have any more contact with Hawk . . . if they try to help him in any way . . . the same thing will happen to them." He grabbed the girl's chin, tipped her head back to stare into her eyes. "Man, woman, boy, or *girl*. Understand?"

The girl's eyes hardened.

Flagg squeezed her chin until she winced. Eyes shifting away from him, she nodded. Flagg dropped his hand. She turned to the crowd and, hanging her head, muttered the warning in Spanish before pushing through the crowd and walking eastward along the street.

The others watched her for a time. Then, casting anxious looks at Flagg and the unconscious Rojas, they slowly dispersed and began shuffling back to their homes. The old crone with the bloody apron crossed herself and set off after the girl.

Flagg turned to the other lawmen, who'd gathered around him, watching the villagers disappearing into the quickly falling night shadows.

Houston said, "What next, Marshal?"

Flagg turned to peer along the trail rising beyond the fountain. "Stable the horses and spread out. Each take a roof top and don't plan on getting any sleep tonight."

"You think he'll come to us?" Miller said, skeptical.

"Now that he knows we're here, you bet I do. Patience isn't one of his virtues."

When the others had drifted off to take up their positions, Flagg continued to stare along the western trail, quickly fading as the night slid down from the ridges and the first stars kindled.

He fished a cheroot from his shirt pocket, bit off an end, stuck it into his mouth, and fired a match.

Puffing smoke, he glanced at Rojas, still lying motionless on his back. The man's breath sounded like a breeze in dry grass, the blood on his face glistening in the last light.

Flagg turned, mounted the boardwalk, and pushed through the batwings. The saloon was dark and empty. No sign of the barman.

Flagg grabbed his whiskey bottle, then sat at a table in the right rear corner. He set his revolver on the table before him and poured himself a drink.

An hour later, on the dark street, Palomar Rojas opened his eye. Gradually, he straightened his legs, wincing and grunting with the effort and at the pain in his cracked ribs.

Blood had dried on his face, making a gummy crust in the corners of his mouth. His head throbbed wickedly, and he squinted his eye against it.

With great effort, taking pinched breaths to keep his ribs from screaming and sending a red haze before his retina, he turned over onto his belly and heaved up on his hands and knees. He grimaced as pain lanced his battered head and nausea rolled through him.

Through a haze of blurred memories, he remembered Flagg tossing away his .36 Colt. He looked around for it, but the street was too dark—there was only a sickly looking light in the saloon's front window—and he couldn't see much of anything but a few nearby horse plops and strewn hay. Behind him loomed the stone fountain.

Again wincing as pain lanced his skull and tore through his ribs, Rojas put one hand and knee in front of the other and crawled toward the saloon.

He arrived at the west end of the saloon's front stoop after nearly two minutes of painful crabbing through the dry dust and manure. At the near corner, he paused and took as deep a breath as he could endure. Then he grunted as he started out again, moving through the small stones, brush, and scattered trash along the warehouse's west side.

Goatheads and sharp pebbles poked his hands and knees, but the pricks were mere annoyances compared to the misery in the rest of him.

A breeze gusted, blowing grit in his eye. Somewhere, an unlatched door tapped its frame. Ahead, two tiny copper lights blazed, then slid to the left as the cat bounded off behind a stable.

Breath whistling through his broken teeth, Rojas crawled around behind the saloon, swinging wide of a woodpile and a privy. Just beyond, four log brush-roofed cribs crouched in the brush and scrub oaks—whores' cribs left over from the boom, when they were occupied every night, with drunk miners lined up in the alley outside, smoking and waiting their turn with Rosa or Maggie or Lorelei or Kate.

The cribs were dark and grown up with weeds. One's roof had collapsed. Rojas had moved into the one farthest east—Kate's digs. Oh, the times he'd had there! After the boom, Kate had moved on, and Rojas had heard she'd succumbed to syphilis somewhere up north.

The old bandito crawled slowly toward the crib, spitting

flecks of dried blood from his lips, grunting and groaning at the constant misery wracking his old body. At the shack's plank door, he rose up on his knees, clutching one arm to his battered ribs, and flipped the latch handle.

When the door screeched open, he dropped to all fours again, crawled inside and plucked a spare Colt from a coffee can on the floor beneath the room's single cot. Holding the pistol in one hand, he cursed and grunted as he pulled himself onto the cot and lay gently down on his back.

"Ay-eee!" he cried softly through his gritted, broken teeth as the cracked ribs shifted.

A crock jug of sangria stood on a small shelf to his left. He grabbed it, uncorked it, lifted his head slightly, and took a long drink. He savored the fruity burn, felt the thick wine instantly begin to cast its spell against his misery.

Squeezing the Colt in one hand, the jug in the other, Rojas lay back against the feed sack he used for a pillow.

He allowed himself a chuckle in spite of the Apache arrows it fired against his ribs. "You should have killed me when you had the chance, you fucking gringo bastard." He took a long pull from the bottle, ran his thumb across the Colt's hammer. "You really should have killed old Palomar!"

He chuckled again, sucked a sharp breath, and stretched his lips back from his teeth.

13.

HOUSE OF CARDS

GIDEON Hawk moved slowly down the northern ridge, keeping as much as possible to the shadows of the cabin-sized boulders and scrub thickets. Occasionally, an old prospector's cabin, abandoned to the winds and the mountain lions, rose up out of the gravel, its brush roof either fallen inside the cabin walls or sprouting tall, brown sod and dried-up flowers.

He was three-quarters of the way down the mountain when the brow of the ridge pulled back, revealing the entire village nestled in the canyon. Hawk hunkered down behind a dilapidated horse stable and cast his gaze down the ridge.

From here he could see mainly rooftops. Here and there on the boulder-strewn slopes flanking the main street and the tiny square, wan lamplight shone in shack windows.

Main Street itself was dark, starlight playing across facades.

Hawk squeezed his Henry rifle in his gloved right hand, ran his left across his jaw. Since Palomar Rojas had informed him of the gringo lawmen's sudden appearance in Bedlam, dread and frustration had gnawed at his gut. It seemed impossible that anyone could have tracked him here, but if anyone could—if there was anyone so determined—that man was D.W. Flagg.

Nothing like political ambitions to spur a man to action.

Hawk had considered waiting at the hacienda for Flagg and his six deputies to come to him. But then he'd decided that if they came to the hacienda, he'd probably have little choice but to kill them all. He had no desire to kill lawmen. Bringing the fight to them was playing into their hands, but it also gave him more control. This way he might not have to kill them. He might be able to discourage a few, send them lifting dust for home.

And then, of course, there was Juliana. He doubted Flagg would hurt the girl, but the possibility wouldn't let him go. He had to make sure.

Hefting the rifle, Hawk rose and continued moving down the ridge, tracing a zigzagging path around brush, boulders, abandoned shacks, and old mine pits. He angled left along the slope, heading for the shack of Juliana and her guardian, Carmelita.

Ten minutes later, he crouched behind a piñon bush flanking Carmelita's small mud-and-brick chicken coop. The chickens had gone to roost, and he could hear them milling and clucking inside. Forty yards away, the tile-roofed shack crouched in the rocky yard, its shutters still open to the cool night air. The brick chimney trickled smoke, tingeing the yard with the spicy smell of chicken stew and tortillas.

Inside, Carmelita spoke in admonishing tones. Hawk knew a good bit of Spanish, but the woman's voice was muffled by the shack's thick walls. He was about to rise and leave when the shack's back door squawked open. Silhouetted by guttering light from a beehive fireplace stood a curvaceous, long-haired figure in a long skirt and serape.

Juliana.

Holding a dishpan in both hands, she strode several paces out from the door, then tossed dishwater onto a spindly ironwood shrub. She began to turn back toward the shack, but stopped. She stood silently, holding the pan in one hand, staring toward the dark mountain rising behind Hawk.

Had she seen him? No. She was no doubt listening for gunfire from the direction of the hacienda.

Hawk resisted the urge to go to her. He wanted to comfort and reassure her, but going to her now might only attract trouble to her and Carmelita. Knowing she was unharmed was enough. When Flagg and the other lawmen were either gone or dead, he'd hold her one last time and tell her good-bye.

Obviously, he couldn't stay in Bedlam. If Flagg had found him, others would, too. Even half-believing he could make a permanent home here with Juliana had been a foolish dream.

She stood near the open door, staring at the mountain. Hawk watched her, his heart heavy, willing her to go back inside and close and lock the door behind her. Finally, a stocky shadow moved in the doorway, and Carmelita ordered her inside.

Juliana jerked with a start. She turned sharply and, casting one last fleeting glance behind her, went inside and closed the door.

Hawk stared at the door for a few seconds. Squeezing his Henry, he rose and began moving back the way he'd come, his heart feeling like a large rock in his chest. When he came to a mine pit a hundred yards up the sloping ridge, he turned left and made his way westward along the slope, paralleling the village on his left but keeping to the shadows. Flagg was no doubt waiting for him, not taking any chances, so he probably had his men posted in every nook and cranny of the canyon.

He was moving down the hill toward the saloon when he heard a breath rattle in a throat. A soft sound, barely audible above the crickets and the breeze shuttling dry leaves along the ground.

Hawk froze. Listening, he held his breath.

A sigh rose from the direction of the crib ahead and to the right. Rojas's crib. Shit, he hoped that old reprobate hadn't returned to the village.

Stealing up to the crib's east wall, he stopped. Inside, someone drank from a crock jug, the liquid sloshing and bubbling. Lips smacked. Another sigh and a low, Spanish curse.

Hawk loosed a curse of his own and stepped up to the door. "Rojas?"

The raspy breathing stopped for a second. Then a chuckle. "I am not taking callers this evening, Senor Hawk."

Hawk tripped the latch and opened the door, slipped inside, and closed it behind him. Rojas hadn't lit a candle, but Hawk's eyes had already adjusted to the darkness. The old bandito lay upon the cot against the right wall, clutching a jug to his chest. His head was propped on a pair of greasy buckskins. His chest rose and fell shallowly. The musty room was rife with the smell of sangria.

Hawk moved to the cot and stared down. "What the hell happened?"

Rojas chuckled again tightly. "I did not take your advice. Instead of slipping off into the mountains for a couple of days, I decided, at my age, that I wasn't going to run from a half dozen yanqui star toters."

"You went back to the saloon."

Rojas opened a hand. "I did not think I'd been followed."

"Idiot." Hawk knelt down beside the cot. "You deserve what you got, you stupid bastard. How bad you hurt?"

"He is bigger than me, and twenty years younger. I think he cracked a couple of ribs."

"Flagg?"

Rojas nodded, then offered the jug to Hawk, who shook his head. Rojas tipped up the jug and took a long pull. Twin streams of wine trickled into his thin, gray chin whiskers. "What are you doing here, amigo?"

"It's Friday night. I came for the saloon dance."

Rojas chuckled. "You aren't long for this world, gringo. There are seven of them and . . . I don't think they like you."

"Where's Flagg?"

"Last I saw, he was heading for the saloon. He'd ordered the others to spread out around the town." Rojas took another drink and sighed, spraying a fine wine vapor on his breath. "You better go back to the hacienda. Better wait for daylight if you're going to fight. I should be on my feet by then. I will help. I'll shoot Flagg's pecker off for you . . . out of the goodness of my heart."

"Shut up and go to sleep."

"Wait." Rojas grabbed Hawk's arm. "Where are you going?"

"I told you."

"Since you don't have long to live, will you do me two simple favors? Wrap my ribs and roll me a cigarette?"

Hawk snorted, set his rifle against the cot, and dug his makings sack from his shirt pocket. The old bandito had plagued the border country for years—mostly as a cattle rustler—but he was no cold-blooded killer. He hadn't thrown a long loop for years and, like Hawk, was only looking for a little peace and quiet here in Bedlam. Hawk couldn't help befriending the oldster. They'd spent many lonely nights in the saloon together, playing cribbage and poker.

When he'd poked the quirley between the old man's sun-cracked lips, and fired it, he helped him out of his bloodstained shirt. He tore the shirt in two, then wrapped it tightly around the old man's waist, Rojas sighing and cursing and puffing cigarette smoke, a fresh sheen of sweat popping out on his forehead. When Hawk had finished tying the knot, Rojas released a long, relieved sigh.

"Ah, amigo," he said, lying back against the breeches and cradling his jug like an infant, "I miss you already!"

"Thanks for the vote of confidence." Hawk picked up his rifle, cracked the door, and peered outside.

There was only the breeze rustling the rabbit brush and

shuffling trash around the shrubs and boulders. High in the mountains, a wildcat screamed.

Hawk turned back to Rojas. *"Hasta luego."* He slipped outside and softly latched the door behind him.

Flagg stood at the front of the saloon, angled so that he could peer westward along the main street toward the fountain and the little square. Behind him, a lantern burned low enough that the dark, dust-streaked window before him did not reflect its glow.

Nothing out there but the dark street, however. Occasionally the breeze blew up hay and dust and skidded it a few feet before spraying it against an abandoned building or corral.

Flagg fingered the Winchester in his right hand. What did he think he was going to see? Hawk wasn't going to mosey up to the saloon and announce himself before he started shooting.

He might not even come tonight. Or any night, for that matter. He might wait for Flagg and the deputies to visit him at his hacienda. Hell, while Flagg was sitting here smoking and sipping whiskey and building his house of cards while listening to the broken-nosed bartender moaning upstairs and squawking his bedsprings, Hawk was probably enjoying good carne asada and a bottle of wine from the hacendado's cellar.

On the other hand, he might be relying on that very train of thought. Taking advantage of it, he might be crabbing up to the saloon at this very moment, his .44 cocked and aimed.

A faint, wooden scrape sounded to Flagg's right. He jumped with a start and snapped his rifle up.

Under a nearby chair, a large rat dropped the bread crust it'd been nibbling and shrieked. It turned and scuttled into the shadows at the back of the room, its toenails scratching the worn puncheons with an eerie rustling.

Flagg glanced around the dark room, as if to make sure no one had seen him. He sucked a deep breath, cast another glance at the night-cloaked street, then lowered the rifle, strode back to his table, and sat down, careful not to nudge the table and tumble the house of cards he'd built from half a poker deck.

He sipped whiskey from his shot glass, then set the glass on the table and picked up the deck. He studied the foot-high house, thumbed a pasteboard from the deck. He placed it on the upper right rear corner of the house and drew his hand away slowly.

A crunching sound rose to his left. His hand jerked slightly, nudging the three of hearts.

The house swayed for a second before the three of hearts tumbled into the six of spades, causing a chain reaction, and the entire house tumbled to the table, clicking and fluttering around Flagg's whiskey bottle and shot glass.

Flagg's eyes weren't on the scattered cards. He was staring at the window to his left. The crunch had sounded outside, around the base of the east wall. His heart fluttered.

Another rat? It sounded like a foot stepping on gravel.

Flagg sat frozen, staring at the dark window, listening.

A silhouette appeared in the window—the profile of a man's head clad in a broad-brimmed, low-crowned hat.

Flagg jerked to his right, blew out the lamp, grabbed his rifle off the chair beside him, and threw himself to the floor. He rolled off his shoulder and hip and pressed his back to the bar. He squeezed the rifle in his hands, poked his right index finger through the trigger guard, and sat frozen, jaws hard, awaiting a shot.

Silence.

Flagg looked at the window. It was an opaque, inky, rectangular blotch. If the figure was still there, Flagg couldn't see it.

Using the rifle butt, he pushed himself to his feet. Casting his glance at the windows around the room, he moved slowly to the front, peered out the windows on both sides of the door, then pushed the left batwing door open with his left hand. The right one he nudged with his rifle barrel.

He stepped slowly through the doors, sidled left, pressed his back against the wall, and looked around.

Nothing but the wind nudging chain-mounted shingles up and down the street, and the two rows of dilapidated shops shouldering against the stars. A tumbleweed rolled down the middle of the street and hung up against a feed trough. Somewhere, a lamb bleated, and farther back in the mountains, coyotes yammered.

The tinny clatter of a kicked can rose on his left. Flagg tightened his hand on the rifle's trigger. His heart thudding, he leapt off the end of the boardwalk and aimed his Winchester toward the building's rear.

The gap between the saloon and an abandoned adobe was murky with shadows and the faint lines of both buildings' outside walls. Spying no movement, Flagg resisted the urge to snap off a couple shots. The figure he'd seen in the window might have belonged to one of the deputies.

He doubted it, but he couldn't take the chance. He could call out, but only at the risk of giving away his position . . . and looking like a fool if it turned out he was only seeing phantoms.

He was going to be damn glad to get Hawk's head on a chopping block.

He released a long breath he hadn't realized he'd held.

Damn glad . . .

Slowly, Flagg rose, feeling sweat trickle into his beard despite the chill wind blowing from the west. Holding the rifle straight out from his left hip, he took a breath, swallowed, and began moving into the darkness between the buildings.

14.

GUNSMOKE AND STARLIGHT

FLAGG'S boots crunched gravel as he moved into the fog of darkness toward the saloon's rear. It was the same sound he'd heard inside a few minutes ago.

A man had been out here, walking around. If it had been one of the deputies, the man would have shown himself by now.

It could have been the barman, Baskin.

Flagg blinked sweat from the corner of his right eye, felt the dampness inside his gloves as he squeezed the rifle's forestock with his right hand. Turning around the saloon's east corner, he moved into the even heavier darkness of the back alley. Directly behind the saloon stood a single brick privy at the base of boulders that had tumbled down from the northern ridge and been sheathed in rabbit brush and gnarled piñons and junipers.

Flagg smelled a trap. It was time to call the deputies. He couldn't take Hawk down alone. He liked the sound of it, liked how it would look in the papers, but only a fool would try.

He tried to speak, but words wouldn't rise from his dry,

tight throat. Fear held them tight in his chest. One sound from his lips would make him an instant target.

Stiffly, sucking shallow breaths through his mouth, he walked between the privy and a pile of stacked pine and mesquite to the far corner of the building, then stopped, staring up along the far side toward the street. He ran his gaze back to the building's rear, where a narrow, crumbling awning slanted toward the alley.

A timbered door stood half-open. In a second-story room on the building's far side, a lamp burned in a window. The smell of mesquite smoke tinged the breeze.

Relief began to loosen the muscles in Flagg's neck. Baskin had come downstairs for wood from the stack flanking the door. It had been the barman's hatted profile in the window.

Vague disappointment followed close on the heels of Flagg's relief. He lowered the rifle slightly, continued walking slowly toward the street.

He hadn't taken two steps before a Spanish-accented voice rose behind him. "Taking some air, Senor Flagg?"

Flagg whipped around, bringing the Winchester to his shoulder. In the shadows to the right of the privy, a match flared, flickered as a hand closed around it. Smoke puffed in the darkness.

"Rojas?"

"Sí." The Mexican's voice was pinched slightly with pain. "I, too, decided to take some air. It is a lovely evening, and fresh air—she is good for an old man's battered body, uh?"

As Flagg moved toward him, Rojas's figure took shape, sitting on a boulder next to the privy, an old-model pistol wedged behind the waistband of his breeches. The bandito leaned back against another, taller rock, one boot hiked on a knee.

He had a pinched look on his wizened face as he stuck the brown-paper quirley to his lips. The coal glowed bright in the darkness.

Flagg kept his rifle aimed at him. "How long you been out here?"

Rojas smiled knowingly. "Not so long, senor."

"You seen anyone—?"

A cold-steel voice rose behind Flagg, cutting off his question: "Only me."

Flagg froze. Blood surged in his ears, and the arteries in his neck throbbed. He stared straight before him. Rojas stared back at him, the old man's thin, chapped lips stretching a grin, his single eye flashing.

Behind Flagg, a boot crunched gravel.

Flagg wheeled, swinging the rifle around and crouching, pulling his index finger back against the trigger as he saw the tall, broad-shouldered figure before him.

Flagg's rifle cracked, flashing and roaring. An eye wink later, the steel-plated Russian in Hawk's right hand spoke, stabbing flames.

The bullet seared through Flagg's right arm, plowing through bone—a burning, tearing pain. Jerking sideways with a grunt, Flagg dropped the rifle and fell to his right knee. He clapped a hand over the bloody hole just above his elbow and turned his head back toward Hawk.

The Colt in Hawk's left hand flashed. The bullet tore through Flagg's left arm, in nearly the same place as on the other.

"Uh-ahhh!"

Gritting his teeth, Flagg stumbled back, fell, and hit the ground on his butt. Blood flowed from both arms, the misery setting his entire body on fire and dropping a veil of exploding fireworks over his eyes.

Holding both pistols straight out before him, Gideon Hawk stared down at the wounded marshal. Flagg writhed before him, cursing and crossing his bloody arms on his chest, clamping the wounds in his hands, the blood oozing between his fingers.

"You crazy son of a bitch!"

Rojas shuffled toward Hawk, grinning down at Flagg.

Hawk jerked his head at the old bandito. "I told you to stay put!"

"It's not every day I get to witness such sweet justice, amigo."

"You've witnessed enough. Go back to your crib before I pump one into you."

Rojas had lifted his chin and turned his head to one side, listening as shouts rose in the night. Running footsteps grew louder. "You better, too, before more powder smoke obscures the stars."

Rojas turned and limped off into the shadows behind the privy.

Hawk sneered at the marshal. "Go home, Flagg. Take your men with you. You'll only get them killed." He turned, grabbed his rifle from the rock he'd set it against, and strode off into the alley's western shadows. "I won't give you another chance."

Movement caught his eye, and he looked toward the saloon's rear stoop, A man ran around the corner, vagrant light flashing off the rifle in his hands. "Hold it!"

"It's him!" Flagg raged, kicking his legs while holding both arms. "*Kill* the son of a bitch!"

The deputy raised his rifle. It flashed and barked, lighting the alley briefly, the report glittering in Flagg's gray, pain-etched eyes. Hawk ducked as the slug spanged off the boulder six inches to his left, spraying rock shards and whistling in his ears.

Bolting behind the boulder, he ran up the gradually rising ridge, weaving around scarps, mesquite and cedar snags, an old chicken coop, and the collection of ancient, abandoned adobes that seemed to be as much a part of the ridge as the rocks and shrubs.

Behind him he could hear the deputies yelling, Flagg shouting curses and orders.

Hawk ducked down behind a heap of old mine tailings a hundred yards above the saloon, and held the Henry across his chest, waiting.

•　　•　　•

Flagg was raging.

Hound-Dog, crouched beside him, held him down with a firm hand on his shoulders, so the man didn't thrash out every ounce of blood from his body.

"After him, goddamnit! What the hell are you waiting for? *After him!* He ran up the ridge, probably heading for his fucking *lair!*"

"Hold still," urged Tuttle. "For Chrissakes, you're gonna—"

As he kicked his legs like an enraged child, Flagg's eyes blazed up at Press Miller. "That's an order! Kill that son of a bitch!"

Miller, crouched around Flagg with the others, his face showing exasperation and revulsion at the blood leaking out both of the marshal's arms, glanced at Hound-Dog. "Get him inside. The rest of us'll try and overtake Hawk."

"I want every man on his trail!" Flagg bellowed.

"Marshal, you're in shock," Miller said reasonably, fingering his rifle's receiver. Having seniority over the other deputies, he was the second-in-command. "If we leave you here untended, you're gonna bleed out. Hound-Dog's had some medical experience. I'm gonna leave him here with you."

As Flagg kicked his right boot savagely, insisting that Hound-Dog go, too, Miller glanced at the others, jerked his head, then rose and strode into the shadows. The other four deputies followed, holding their rifles high in both hands as they traced Hawk's course around the scarp and headed up the ridge.

Hound-Dog looked down at Flagg.

The marshal winced and bellowed, cursing, casting his gaze from one bloody arm to the other. "Thought I'd turn tail." He chuckled crazily. "I'm gonna *kill* that son of a bitch!"

Hound-Dog ripped his neckerchief off, began looping it over Flagg's right arm. "Don't waste your energy, Marshal. Soon as I get your arms wrapped, I'll take you inside and

try to figure out how much damage that crazy bastard did
to ye."

When Tuttle had both of Flagg's arms wrapped with
neckerchiefs, he slipped his hands under the marshal's
arms, tugging him to his feet. He had to do most of the lifting. Flagg was growing weak from blood loss and shock.

One arm around the man's waist, Tuttle led Flagg to the
saloon's back door, then inside and up the stairs at the back
of the main hall. The second-story hallway was dark, but a
thin line of light beneath a door at the far end revealed five
other doors. Choosing one at random, Tuttle threw it open
and led Flagg inside to a bed.

Flagg sagged onto the mattress, the leather springs
complaining. He froze when the muffled cracks of a rifle
sounded, rending the quiet night. The six or seven shots
seemed to have been fired by the same rifle.

Flagg glanced at Tuttle, who'd frozen beside him,
shaggy eyebrows arched as he listened. Snarling, the marshal grabbed the big deputy's broad arm and squeezed,
gritting his teeth. "Go find out what's going on, Hound-
Dog. I want to know what's going *on*!"

He'd no sooner bellowed the last word than his eyes
grew heavy. The snarl faded from his lips, and his shoulders slumped, as if the muscles and tendons had suddenly
dissolved.

"Easy, Marshal." Hound-Dog eased the man down onto
the bed. It wasn't hard. Flagg was almost out, his breath
growing shallow, eyelids fluttering.

Behind Tuttle, a door latch clicked. He rose quickly,
wheeling toward the room's open door as he drew his Colt
Army from the cross-draw holster on his left hip, raking
the hammer back.

Near the doorway, keeping close to the hall's far wall,
the barman appeared in his canvas breeches and underwear
shirt, suspenders hanging down his sides. He held a rusty
bull's-eye lantern up high in his right hand.

Lowering the pistol, Tuttle said, "The marshal's been
hurt. There a sawbones in town?"

Baskin raised the lamp a little higher as he moved forward and peered into the room. The copper lantern's light fell across Flagg's bloody, unconscious body. The barman's own eyes were swollen nearly shut. That and his broad, purple nose gave him a bizarre, owl-like look.

He glanced at Tuttle, pursing his lips with satisfaction. He snorted, "No," then turned and sauntered back down the hall. Shortly, a door closed and latched with a solid thud.

His own breath coming hard and raspy from enervation, Hound-Dog peered around the dark room, found a gas lamp on the dresser, and lit it. With his bowie knife, he'd cut away both of Flagg's bloody sleeves and was examining the wounds when voices rose from the alley.

The voices moved inside, echoing around the main hall and obscured by boots pounding the floorboards then hammering the stair steps and growing louder, making the entire building shake.

Press Miller's face appeared in the doorway. He was sweating and breathing hard, his hat askew. He shook his head as he stepped into the room.

"He fired at us from up the ridge. There's no way we can take him in the dark. He knows the terrain too well."

The others filed in behind him and spread out around the bed. Miller shuttled his gaze from Flagg to Tuttle. "How's he look?"

By way of answer, Tuttle spoke to the group, urgency pitching his voice. "I need my saddlebags from the livery barn. I also need hot water, whiskey, and all the cloth you can find." He glanced at Villard. "Franco, I'll be needin' your stiletto to dig those bullets out."

All the other men except Miller and Villard shuffled out of the room and down the stairs. Villard hiked his right boot onto a chair, jerked his trouser cuffs above his boots, and slid a slender, bone-handle stiletto from the well.

As Villard handed the knife to Tuttle, Flagg opened his eyes. They were red-rimmed and rheumy, spoked with pain lines. His glance found Miller staring down at him.

Flagg cleared phlegm from his throat, curled his upper lip. "You get him, Press?"

"First thing in the mornin'," Miller said. His nostrils flared. "When you open your eyes tomorrow, first thing you'll see is Hawk's head starin' at you from that washstand over there."

Flagg sneered and grunted as misery shot through him. His eyes held on Miller's. "Tough talk. You make good on it . . . or I'll see you only work as a deputy *town* marshal in a backwater *mining* camp."

Tuttle and Miller shared a glance. Then, his face flushed, Miller turned, hefted his rifle, and went out.

15.

THE HUNTED

AFTER he'd fired a half dozen shots at the deputies climbing the ridge behind him, giving them second thoughts about the night scout, Hawk returned to the hacienda. He quickly stuffed his saddlebags and war bag with his possibles, then saddled his horse and made a dry camp a hundred yards east along the ridge.

In a slight cleft in the ridge, the ruins of an old stone house—probably an ancient sheepherder's shack—stood amidst brush and rocks and sparse firs and pines. Just east of the shack, an arroyo ran down the ridge toward the canyon, choked with mesquite, paloverde trees, cactus, desert willows, and a few spindly cottonwoods. It was a direct route down to the village, but, with the dense cholla, "jumping cactus," it was no place for horses. The few times Hawk had felt like walking instead of riding to the village for supplies, he'd discovered several mine pits along the wash, as well as a dozen or so Apache arrows, two of which protruded from a half-mummified man in threadbare dungarees and hobnailed boots, a few strands of long red hair curling atop his head.

Hawk spent the night sitting with his back to the shack's

ruined west wall, holding his Henry across his thighs. He took catnaps while keeping an eye and ear skinned on the hacienda hulking in the western darkness, which was where Flagg's men would no doubt look when they came stalking him.

It was doubtful any would turn back. It was their job to bring him in or, as the governors' death warrant provided, to kill him.

They'd been his colleagues at one time, so he'd felt compelled to warn them off. He'd given them a chance to turn around and go home. If they didn't—if they insisted, instead, on continuing the hunt—he had no choice but to turn and fight.

No animal—grizzly, wolf, mountain lion, or man— could be expected to do otherwise.

The stars turned in the velvet sky. Nightbirds called. His bedroll draped about his shoulders, warding off the early autumn chill, Hawk slept and woke, slept and woke. Once, he rose, stretched, and strolled around the shack as he smoked. When he'd finished the cigarette, he drained his bladder and sat back down against the wall.

He yawned and draped the blankets around his shoulders, set the rifle across his thighs. The cold seeped up from the ground. The rifle barrel grew chill. He yearned for a bed. This hunted life was getting old, but now that the wheel was spun, there was no way to stop it save death.

That time would come. But not before he'd taken down a few more killers like those who'd killed Jubal. Not before the men hunting him had earned their trophy.

He leaned his head back against the cold stone wall. Shortly, his eyes grew heavy, and his chin dipped to his chest.

Later, he became aware of warm air caressing him. A wren chittered. Hawk opened his eyes and looked around, curling his finger through the Henry's trigger guard.

The trees and brush stood silhouetted against a paling sky. Gray light pooled atop stones, filling their pits and fissures with purple shadows, and squirrels scuttled along pine branches.

Hawk remained sitting, moving only his eyes, taking in everything around him, looking for hidden dangers he might have missed while he slept. Deeming the area safe, he was reaching for his canteen when a squirrel suddenly began yammering loudly down the arroyo, as if scolding an interloper.

The cacophony cut through the morning silence, making Hawk's pulse race.

He climbed to his feet stiffly, moved to the shack's front corner, and dropped to one knee, peering down the arroyo.

There was the faint click of a kicked stone.

Hawk raised the Henry to his shoulder, snugged his cheek against the stock. He aimed down the V-shaped notch obscured by overhanging branches. A few seconds later, a figure moved toward him, barely seen behind the veil of leaves and pine trunks.

Anticipating the man's route, Hawk aimed at a gap between two branches, and waited. Footsteps rose. The figure appeared between the branches, the head moving into Hawk's rifle sights. His finger tensed on the trigger, began taking up the slack.

Seeing the long hair and curved figure, his heart thudded. He flicked his finger away from the trigger, and lowered the rifle, squinting down the arroyo.

The girl ducked under a pine branch and moved into the open, shoulders hunched beneath a frayed, brown serape.

Hawk kept his voice low. "Juliana!"

She stopped suddenly, turned to him, her hair flying about her shoulders. "Gideon?"

Hawk rose and tramped quickly down the arroyo and grabbed her arm. "What the hell are you doing here?"

Face flushed from the climb, eyes worried, she looked up at him. "There are lawmen in the village. Last night, I heard the shooting. I had to come."

"You shouldn't have."

"I kept imagining you up here alone, dying." She threw

her arms around him, burying her head in his chest. "But you are all right?"

He pushed her away from him, kept one hand on her arm. "Damnit, they might have seen you, followed you!"

"I was very cautious."

Hawk cast his gaze down the arroyo. The squirrel had stopped its tirade for a time. Now, it had started again. Far down the arroyo, Hawk thought he spied movement through the branches.

"I'm getting you out of here." He turned and, jerking Juliana along behind him, tramped back up the arroyo and around the shack to where he'd tied the grulla. He'd send her back to town via the main trail.

"Gideon, I am sure I was not followed—"

Hawk stopped suddenly, staring northwest. Thirty yards away, the grulla was walking away from him . . . being *led* away from him by a man in a long gray duster and black, high-crowned hat.

Hawk's heart lurched. "Run!"

He pushed the girl forward, and turned back the way he'd come. Twenty yards away, smoke puffed under a willow and a rifle cracked, the slug spanging off a rock half a foot before Hawk's right boot, spraying gravel in his face.

Behind him, Juliana screamed. He heard her stumble and fall.

Rage burning through him, Hawk slammed the Henry's butt against his right hip, aimed down the arroyo, and snapped off a veritable fusillade, blowing up dust and snapping branches and punching bullets through cactus plants.

Amidst the cracks of the Henry, a man grunted. Several others shouted angrily.

Hawk snapped the rifle up and turned, looking for the deputy who'd been leading the grulla off. The horse was nowhere in sight. The deputy was hunkered down behind a deadfall pine, his cheek snugged against a rifle stock, the barrel aimed at Hawk.

Hawk wheeled as the rifle boomed. The slug slammed

into a mesquite branch as Hawk bolted forward. Juliana was on the ground, staring up at him, terrified. Hawk grabbed her arm as several more shots split the air around him. He pulled her up and over the ridge behind the sheep-herder's shack, the deputies' shots kicking up dust and pummeling stones at their heels.

The shots continued angrily as Hawk and Juliana ran down the opposite ridge, Hawk clutching her hand in his own. Several slugs spanged off the ridge crest, careening harmlessly into the air, before the shooting stopped alto-gether.

When Hawk and Juliana had followed a game path through the chaparral for a hundred yards, another rifle boomed on the ridge top. Hawk didn't turn around but kept running, pulling the girl around a trail bend.

The slug blasted rock to their right.

Then they were scrambling down the ridge and into the canyon. The stream where they'd fished was a meandering, silver thread in the misty morning shadows at the bottom of the gorge.

When several more shots sounded, and excited shouts lifted, Hawk stopped. "Keep going!"

As Juliana kept running down the switchbacking trail, Hawk turned and aimed the Henry up toward the ridge crest. The deputies were following the trail in a shaggy line, running. Hawk planted a bead on the first man, and fired.

The slug tore into a stunt cedar behind him, the shot echoing around the canyon. The man dove into the brush as Hawk levered a fresh shell and fired at the man behind him.

That shot, too, was errant. The man dropped behind a boulder while the others behind him scrambled for cover farther up the ridge.

Hawk rose and ran after Juliana.

He'd gone ten yards when the deputies' shots resumed, spanging off the rocks around him, spraying sand and shards, ricocheting around his legs and snapping cedar branches.

He'd nearly caught up to the girl when he stopped again, swinging around while raising the Henry toward his shoulder. A bullet slammed into the Henry's breech with an ear-numbing scream, sending sparks into his eyes, the ricochet tearing across his right hand. The rifle tumbled out of his hands, smoking.

Hawk lunged toward it. Two slugs blasted into the rocks before him. He pulled back, glanced up trail.

The deputies were closing, pausing only to fire.

As three shots hammered around him, Hawk turned. Leaving the Henry and cursing his luck—he was armed now with only two revolvers against six men with rifles—he ran after Juliana's retreating figure.

He overtook her as they gained the canyon bottom. Not slowing down, he grabbed her arm. They ran east along the gurgling stream, the deputies' shots whistling over their heads and pounding the opposite ridge.

Hawk and the girl turned a bend in the trail. They leapt the stream and sprinted into the narrow feeder canyon, startling several mule deer grazing the ironwood shrubs.

"Inside!" Hawk ordered when they'd come to the low, oval opening at the base of the canyon wall.

He pushed Juliana through the cave mouth and turned. No sign of the deputies, but shouts echoed from the main chasm. He dropped to all fours, swept his hands across the fresh prints in the chalky dust, then doffed his hat, and rolled through the opening. He crawled until the ceiling rose, then stopped, half-turned back toward the light, and dangled a wrist over a knee.

He could hear better than he could see Juliana in the darkness, breathing heavily. He could feel the heat of her body beside him. Neither of them said anything. In the heavy silence, they listened intently.

Outside, footsteps sounded—boots puffing dry dirt, spurs chinging. "They came this way," said one of the deputies, the voice muffled by ten feet of solid rock.

The sounds faded, then died as the men passed the opening without spying the notch cave. Farther inside the cavern, bat wings flapped, echoing their sinewy squeak, and Hawk felt the fragrant, heavy humidity pushing toward him from the falls.

"They're gone," Juliana said through a long, relieved sigh.

"For now."

Hawk rose, grabbed her hand, and led her back into the chasm. They came to the waterfall and looked around. The sky above the falls was a soft, early morning gray stitched with the small, winged silhouettes of birds. Light tumbled over the rocks of the sunken roof, glittering dully on the water and filling most of the gorge with cool, black shadows.

Hawk stared at the jumble of wet rocks rising to the ceiling. Slippery, no doubt, but climbable.

Hawk took her hand again, led her to the base of the falls. He raised his voice above the clamor of the water on the rocks.

"We're gonna climb out of here. It won't be long before those lawmen find the notch cave, so we have to hurry. You go first. Watch your step!"

Juliana's fear-glazed eyes met his, then moved to the falls. She lifted the heavy serape over her head, tossed it down, then sprang forward into the tumbling stream. Instantly wet and spitting water, she reached up, grabbed a rock, hiked her foot onto another, and began climbing.

Hawk waited until she was six feet above him, then followed her, reaching for holds and dodging the three or four streams of falling water. Juliana rose nimbly above him. Once, she loosed a rock, which tumbled over Hawk's head and clattered onto the floor below.

She stopped and looked down, eyes wide. "Sorry!"

Catching a slender thread of water in his left eye, Hawk made a face and shook his head. "Keep climbing!"

He reached up, grabbed a rock furred with mineral deposits. His hand slipped off the rock, and for a moment he hung by only his right hand. He dug a boot into the wall, found a crevice, and, ignoring his heart's hammering, continued climbing.

Above, Juliana was nearly to the top.

Hawk lowered his head, looked for another handhold, and continued climbing. When he looked up again, he was five feet from the lip of the gorge.

Juliana had disappeared.

Only the spring-fed stream curled over a shelf of black granite and tumbled into the hole, the edge of the stream soaking his left arm and clouding his eyes with vapor.

Hawk bunched his lips and heaved himself up. In seconds, he peered up and over the lip of the chasm.

His stomach sank and filled with bile.

Juliana stood ten feet back from the hole. A tall, patch-bearded man with a moon-and-star badge pinned to his duster lapel stood behind her. He had one arm across her chest, gripping her firmly against him. His other hand held a long-barreled Colt Navy to her temple. Her dress and underclothes were soaked, clinging to every curve.

Two other men stood to each side, aiming Winchesters at Hawk.

The man holding Juliana stretched a taut smile. He lifted a firm, round breast in his gloved right hand. Juliana grimaced and cursed him. He ignored her.

"Nice-lookin' little wench you got here, Hawk." Squeezing Juliana's breast with one hand, Press Miller cocked his pistol with the other, set it firmly against her head. "Climb on out of there real peaceable-like, or I'll kill her."

16.

TROPHY

HAWK ground his teeth as he stared up at Miller. "Let her go."

"Climb out of there, and keep your hands away from your holsters"—Miller pressed the gun barrel harder against Juliana's temple, and she sucked a sharp breath—"or I'll spray her brains all over these rocks."

Hawk placed both hands on the lip of the hole and hoisted his knees up and out. He got his feet under him and stood, keeping his hands away from his revolvers, his eyes locked on Miller. The deputy still had Juliana's left breast in his hand, lifting and squeezing.

"I said let her go."

Miller glared at Hawk. "You ain't givin' the orders here. I'm givin' the orders now, you crazy son of a bitch." He pulled his revolver away from the girl's head, wagged it at Hawk. "Lift out those pistols with two fingers, and toss 'em over here, by my feet. Real slow."

Hawk looked at Juliana. She stared at him, sobbing, tears streaming down her cheeks.

Slowly, he flipped his guns onto a mound of sand to the

right of Miller's boots—even in defeat reluctant to mistreat his weapons.

Miller dipped his chin and smiled at Hawk with guile. "The stiletto."

Hawk reached up behind his head and slid the bone-handled knife from the sheath hanging down his back by a rawhide cord, which his neckerchief concealed. He tossed the razor-edged knife into the sand with the revolvers.

One of the other deputies called up from the bottom of the hole, his voice barely audible above the stream's rush and splash.

"We got him!" Miller shouted back, shoving Juliana to his right, where another deputy—a rangy Texas lawman whom Hawk recognized as Bill Houston—grabbed her while keeping his rifle aimed at Hawk. "We'll meet you back in the main canyon," Miller added.

He glanced at one of the other lawmen and canted his head at Hawk. "Pat him down and tie his hands behind his back. Tie him good. Tie his ankles, too. Just enough rope so he can walk but not run. Bill, do the same with the girl."

"Let her go," Hawk said, as the Cajun, Franco Villard, patted him down from behind. "She's got no part in this."

"Sure as hell does," Miller spat, turning his sharp eyes to the girl. "She climbed that ravine to cavort with a known felon when just last night Flagg warned her not to. Warned the whole damn town."

"She meant no harm."

Miller slitted an eye at Juliana, standing tensely as Houston tied her hands behind her back, her breasts pushing at the wet dress. Miller stretched a wolfish grin. "No girl built like that one is *ever* harmless. Ain't that right, boys?"

They all chuckled. Behind Juliana, eyes lowered to study his work, Houston shook his head. He'd stuck a cold cigar between his teeth.

"Keep your hands off her," Hawk warned Miller as Villard strung a rope between his ankles. His wrists were already tied behind his back. His hard green eyes bored into Miller. "You touch her again, I'll kill you."

Miller's own expression hardened. "Well, now," he growled, stepping toward Hawk. "I reckon your killin' days are over, Mr. Rogue Lawman." He raised his Winchester's barrel, and swung the butt up savagely into Hawk's solar plexus.

The wind left Hawk's chest in a single, loud burst. His knees buckled. He almost fell but got his feet back under him at the last second, his jaw tightening as he fought against the pain and tried to suck air into his lungs.

"Bastard!" Juliana screamed at Miller, lunging toward him. She tripped on the rope tying her ankles together, and fell to her knees. Hands tied behind her back, she shook her hair from her eyes and regarded Miller with fury. "You are a *coward*!"

Miller snapped his head toward her. "Shut up, bitch!"

"Juliana," Hawk rasped, his voice gently chastising. He winced as he sucked a breath.

"I am sorry, Gideon!" Juliana sobbed, chin falling to her chest. "I led them right to you!"

"They would have found me," Hawk said.

"You got that right."

Keeping his rifle on Hawk, Miller stooped to retrieve the revolvers and stiletto near his feet. He wedged both revolvers behind his cartridge belt, slipped the stiletto into the sheath housing his bowie knife, and rose. He stepped aside and wagged his rifle at Hawk and the girl, grinning tensely. "Now, why don't we call on Marshal Flagg? He's feelin' rather poorly, don't you know?"

Bill Houston rolled his cigar to one side of his mouth. "I think he's about to feel a whole lot better real soon!"

Hawk, Juliana, and the deputies followed a narrow, meandering mountain-goat trail down to the main canyon. Along the stream in which Hawk and the girl had fished a couple of days before, they joined up with the other three deputies and climbed the ridge to the sheepherder's ruined shack.

Hawk's horse was tied to a cedar just east of the shack. Miller ordered Juliana into the saddle. He ordered Hawk to lead the horse. Leading the grulla by the reins and having to take short steps because of the rope tied to his ankles, Hawk began making his way slowly back down the arroyo toward the village.

Miller led the procession, walking ten feet in front of Hawk, the Winchester resting on the senior deputy's right shoulder. He strode with his chin proudly lifted, whistling victoriously. The other three walked behind the horse, not saying anything, spurs chinging, boots occasionally kicking stones. Someone was smoking; Hawk could smell the tobacco wafting on the warm, morning breeze.

He stared straight ahead, the buckskin reins in his hands behind his back, the horse clomping at his heels. He was surprised to feel as much relief as defeat.

The running was over.

Juliana hadn't said anything since they'd left the ridge above the cave. Now her voice rose thinly. "Gideon, if it were not for me—"

Miller turned his head to one side. "No talkin' there, girl." He snickered. "Besides, I don't think ole Hawk wants to talk to you no more . . . after you went and got him greased for the pan and all . . ."

Miller chuckled again and turned his head forward as he passed a saguaro towering over the trail to his right.

Hawk turned to Juliana, winked, and continued walking.

When the arroyo opened at the north end of the village, Hawk stopped. Ahead of him, Miller stopped, too, and turned with an angry frown.

"What the hell you think you're doin'?"

"Let her go."

Miller glanced at Juliana sitting the horse behind Hawk. He opened his mouth to speak, but Hawk cut him off.

"She's no threat. You got me. Turn her loose."

"The man's got a point," said Bill Houston as he and Villard walked up on Hawk's right, staying wide and keeping their rifles aimed at the prisoner. The other three lawmen swung to the left. "Why bother with her? We got what we came for."

Miller looked at him, then at Villard, whose expression said he agreed with Houston. Miller jerked his head at the girl. "Cut her loose."

When Houston had cut Juliana's ropes and helped her out of the saddle, she ran to Hawk and threw her arms around him. She pressed her head against his chest. Miller grabbed her arm.

As he pulled her away, she looked up at Hawk, who regarded her stonily. "Go home. Forget about me."

"Good advice," Miller said. "No sense in pinin' for a dead man." He told Villard to take the grulla to the livery barn, then nudged Hawk forward with his rifle barrel.

Hawk glanced at Juliana staring up at him, fresh tears streaking her dusty cheeks and glistening in the sunlight, her arms hanging straight down at her sides. Quickly memorizing every feature of the girl's lovely face, the thick dark hair framing her head and falling about her shoulders, he turned away.

"Gideon."

He ignored the plaintive cry, and walked to the main street with Miller, Houston, and the other three deputies tramping along behind. He turned the corner and did not look back as he headed for Green's Saloon.

His heart hammered slowly. His ears rang. His feet felt as heavy as lead within his boots.

"Inside," Miller said as they approached the saloon, giving Hawk another poke in the back.

"You're proud as a peacock, Press," Hawk said. "Be careful your feathers don't get stepped on."

"Shut up!"

Hawk mounted the porch steps, stumbling over the rope between his ankles, and pushed through the batwings. He crossed the empty saloon and climbed the stairs at the back, the rope forcing him to take one step at a time, not lifting one foot before the other was firmly planted.

He was three-quarters of the way up when, behind him, Miller cursed impatiently and rammed his Winchester into the small of Hawk's back. Hawk's boot toe clipped a riser. He stumbled, dropped to a knee.

He turned, glowering hard over his right shoulder. His nostrils flared. His green eyes turned to small, hot fires. Miller held his gaze for a moment before the deputy's face colored, and his eyes flicked away like mice looking for a hole.

"We ain't got all day," he muttered.

Hawk continued staring at Miller as he pulled himself to his feet. Then he turned and continued up the stairs, moving slower than before.

At the top, he nudged the left wall and planted his feet. While the other deputies stopped on the stairs behind him, Miller moved past Hawk and knocked on a door on the right side of the hall.

"Come!" Hawk recognized Flagg's taut, hoarse voice behind the door.

Miller, unable to contain another self-satisfied smirk, turned to Hawk, crooked a finger, then threw the door open. He disappeared inside. Hawk continued down the hall, the other deputies' boots pounding behind him.

He turned into the room, and stopped.

On the room's small bed, Flagg reclined against the headboard, his back to the far wall. Both of his heavily bandaged arms were secured with slings made from old bedsheets tied around his neck. He wore a gray underwear top, unbuttoned halfway down his chest, which was matted with wiry gray hair. His face was flushed and sweat-damp. An open bottle rested against his left hip, beside a walnut-butted Remington.

The room smelled of sweat, carbolic acid, wood smoke, and alcohol.

To Flagg's right stood a spool-back chair upon which sat a chessboard. On the other side of the chair sat the saloon's burly proprietor, Leo Baskin, the barman's face swollen around a pear-sized nose as purple as ripe grapes on the vine. He wore a quilted robe over long-handles, and an orange night sock on his head. When Hawk had first entered, Baskin had been resting his forearms on his knees, studying the chess game before him. Now he sat up, eyes registering shock deep within their doughy sockets.

One hand on the whiskey bottle, Flagg glowered up at Hawk.

"That trophy I promised, Marshal," said Miller, leaning back against the dresser to fire a quirley. "Want me to cut his head off, make it easier to take him back to Denver City?"

Flagg's gray-bearded face was stony, but his eyes were sun-fired steel discs. His left hand squeezed the bottle so hard that his knuckles turned white.

"Where'd you get him?"

"Top o' the ridge. He was waitin' for us."

"*How'd* you get him?"

Miller was lighting his quirley, puffing smoke.

"The girl," said Franco Villard.

"Led us up the arroyo," added Bill Houston.

Leaning against the dresser, Miller removed the quirley from his mouth, blew a long stream of smoke, and casually flicked a speck of tobacco from his tongue.

Flagg hadn't taken his eyes off Hawk. "Fire up the telegraph."

Miller glanced at the other deputies, turned his head to Flagg. "There ain't no telegraph here, Marshal. There ain't much of *anything* here."

"We're a week's ride out of Denver City, Marshal," reminded Hound-Dog Tuttle, standing on the far side of Flagg's bed, sweating and breathing hard from the long hike, his rust-colored shirt pasted against his belly. "Maybe we oughta take him to Tucson."

"Hellfire!" Flagg rumbled, his jaws quivering. "We're taking that son of a bitch to Denver. He'll hang over Cherry Creek, with a whole crowd to see."

"And a whole gaggle of Eastern reporters," Hawk said, standing with his feet spread, hands tied behind his back, a knowing light in his eyes. "You can send a cable from Tombstone, have the band playing as our train pulls into Union Station." Hawk shook his head slowly. "If you aren't headed for great things, Flagg, I don't know who is."

"Shut up, you fuckin' bastard!" Flagg roared. "If I had time enough to *drag* you to Denver, I'd put two bullets in you, like you did to *me*."

He turned to Miller. "This place have a jail?"

Miller nodded.

"Lock him up! I want two men on him all night! Tomorrow, at first blush of dawn, we ride for Tombstone!"

"You ain't gonna be fit to ride tomorrow yet," Hound-Dog pointed out, nodding at Flagg's arms.

"Watch me!"

As the deputies ushered Hawk out the door, Hawk stopped and turned his head toward the barman. "Ah, Leo," he said, shuttling his eyes to the chessboard, "you can take his king."

17.

PRETTY GIRL
TRAVELING ALONE

EARLIER that same day, traveling westward on the trail Hawk and the deputies had taken two days earlier, Saradee Jones brought her sleek palomino stallion up a slight rise through high, pine country. She shifted her sore bottom on the saddle, which she'd padded with a red velvet pillow she'd stolen from the parlor of the hotel in which Flagg had beaten her.

She knew where Flagg was heading because she knew where Hawk had headed. She'd followed Hawk to Bedlam before, pulled toward him by some invisible rope she'd sensed connecting them since the first time they'd met.

Only this time it wasn't Hawk she was trailing. This time it was D.W. Flagg.

Getting as comfortable as she could in her situation, she looped her reins around the saddle horn, dipped a hand into the pocket of her blue-checked shirt, and produced a small tobacco pouch. Letting the horse plod slowly along the trail toward the shaded rise, she dug papers from the pouch, troughed one between the index and forefinger of her right hand, and dribbled tobacco into the crease.

She was licking the paper to seal it as the palomino topped the rise and started down the other side, its hooves clomping on the narrow, rocky, sun-dappled trail. Her eyes were canted down to the cigarette when she heard a man laugh on the trail ahead.

Jerking her head up, she dropped the quirley and slapped the butt of the revolver thonged low on her right thigh.

Ahead, four riders were moving toward her up the rise, the pines casting columnar shadows across their shabby trail clothes and dusty stock ponies. Oblivious to her, they were laughing and talking, the lead rider hipped around in his saddle to talk to the three men tightly grouped behind him.

Two seconds after Saradee had slapped her Colt's butt, one of the men riding behind the leader glanced casually up trail, glanced away, then back again, his eyes glinting incredulously as he picked Saradee out of the tree shadows before him.

He spoke in a low voice to the others, then canted his head toward her. The others snapped their own eyes forward, too. Three touched their pistol butts while the fourth—a wiry, red-headed kid in a torn duster and black stovepipe hat—reached for the rifle snugged in the leather saddle sheath under his right thigh.

Saradee kept her own hand on her Colt's grips, leaving the gun in the holster, as the approaching men ran their eyes up and down her long-legged, buxom figure in tight jeans and man's shirt, their expressions softening, the cast in their gazes turning by slow degrees from caution to bemusement to lust.

"Hi, there," the lead rider said as he drew his mount to a halt before Saradee.

Saradee had already checked down the palomino, regarding the four men blandly while her horse stared warily ahead, twitching its ears and rippling its withers.

"To what do we owe the honor?" asked a pudgy gent with a broad, pimpled face framed by wispy muttonchop whiskers. His eyes beneath the brim of his black weather-beaten hat were an odd, washed-out gray.

Saradee blinked, removed her hand from her pistol grips, and swung down from her saddle. "The honor of what?" she said with a fleeting glance at the ragtag group before turning and walking back up the hill, holding the palomino's reins loosely in her gloved left hand. Four feet beyond the horse's bronze-cream tail, she stooped, plucked her cigarette out of the dust, and straightened.

Flicking the quirley lightly across her shirt, cleaning it, she strolled back down the hill toward the group blocking the trail before her.

"The honor of meeting such a pretty girl out here in the middle of nowhere," said the man with the muttonchops and washed-out eyes.

Saradee stuck the cigarette in her mouth, grabbed the horn, and pulled herself into the saddle.

"On such a magnificent horse, too," said the fourth rider—tall, gaunt, and unshaven, a black patch over his left eye and bandoleers crossed on his beaded vest. He was smoking a long, black cheroot, his sole eye squinted cunningly as he appraised the palomino.

Saradee plucked a sulfur match from her pocket and offered a wooden smile. "Charmed."

"Where you headed?" asked the red-headed kid.

Saradee snapped the match to life on her thumbnail. "Bedlam."

"Bedlam?" said Muttonchops. "Bedlam's a ghost town."

"I happen to like ghost towns," said Saradee as she lit the cigarette, puffing smoke. "They're so quiet. Even the ghosts."

The men chuckled, casting their amused, conspiratorial glances back and forth among themselves. The redhead turned his wolfish gaze back to Saradee. "Why don't you forget about that dusty old ghost town. That's no place for a girl like you. Why, you can ride to Tombstone with us!"

"Tombstone?"

"Yeah." The redhead glanced at the tall gent's bulging saddlebags. "We just happened to run across a little fortune . . . by purely legitimate means, of course. We figured on havin' us a good ole hoof-stompin' time in Tombstone with our newfound treasure, drinkin' and gamblin' and such." His brows furrowed suddenly, as if from deep consternation. "Only one thing's been missin'."

"Oh?" Saradee said, matching the man's frown with her own, her voice pitched with mock gravity. "And what thing would that be?"

"Why, a pretty little gal like yourself!" intoned the first rider, smoothing his droopy mustaches with the first two fingers of his gloved left hand. His horse was sniffing the palomino, the palomino lifting its head indignantly.

"Sorry," Saradee said, taking a slow pull on her quirley. "My momma told me to watch out for boys like you."

"Boys like us?" said the first rider, feigning indignance. "Now, what kind of boys would we be?"

"Chowderheaded peckerwoods," Saradee said, matter-of-factly. "Who wouldn't know what to do with a girl like me if I gave you lessons for the next ten years."

She heeled the palomino forward, nudging the first two riders out of her path, their horses sidestepping nervously and chuffing. Smoke puffed out behind her as she trotted the palomino down the hill.

Behind her, the men chuckled uncertainly, brows ridged.

"Won't you reconsider?" shouted the tall man above the clattering of the horses' shod hooves. "The trail ain't safe for a pretty girl travelin' alone!"

"Thanks for the admonition," Saradee called, spurring the palomino into a trot. She cast a glance behind at the four men watching her from the shaded hillside, and smiled, showing her perfect white teeth between her wide, red lips. "I'll keep a finger on my trigger and an eye on my back trail!"

She stopped two hours later atop a rocky knob, and peered into the ravine she'd just left. A half mile east along the ravine's floor, a mare's tail of brown dust curled amidst the saguaros and mesquite shrubs.

Just the right amount of dust for four riders who'd set their hats for a pretty girl and a fine-boned, broad-chested palomino.

"Come on, boys," Saradee said. "Don't be late for supper. I could use some beans and biscuits and I'm about out of coffee, too. Wouldn't mind gettin' my hands on that money in your poke, neither!"

She chuckled and kicked the palomino down the scarp, parting shrubs and heading into a shallow wash twisting between seven-foot-high banks streaked with shale and pocked with swallows' nests.

She traced a gradual bend and paused to watch a thick, Mojave-green rattlesnake twisting up out of its hole in the side of the ridge. Fascinated, she unsheathed her rifle and prodded the snake with the barrel.

It struck, closing its mouth around the steel. With a bewildered cast to its flat, copper-colored eyes, the snake recoiled against the sandstone wall and beat a fast retreat to its hole.

Saradee watched it, her face lit up like an awestruck child's. When the snake had coiled back into its hole, she sheathed her rifle and rode on.

After another hour, she stopped the palomino under a low mesa, the west-falling sun filling the hollow with cool purple shade. A thin, shallow freshet ran along the base of the mesa, sheathed in grama grass and sage.

Saradee cast a look over her right shoulder. Her pursuers were nearly a mile away, walking their horses along the shoulder of a cedar-stippled mountain. She probably wouldn't have noticed them if she hadn't been keeping an eye on them for the past several hours. Each rider was no bigger than the nail on her little finger from this distance, but there they were, just the same. They'd probably lay off until the sun went down, then move in after dark.

Unless she could lure them in sooner.

Saradee dismounted, unsaddled her horse, and tied it to a cedar tree near the little stream. She rubbed the animal down with dry grass, taking her time but keeping an eye on the sun, which had another hour yet before it disappeared behind the western ridges.

When she'd gathered wood for a small fire and spread her bedroll, she cast another glance at the ridge behind her, colored now a deep, brassy orange. She could no longer see the riders, but they could probably see her.

She chewed her lower lip, turned away from the ridge, removed her gun belt, and coiled it atop a nearby boulder. She glanced again behind her, then pulled her shirttails out of her pants and slowly began unbuttoning her shirt, her cool eyes staring at the stream, sensual excitement rippling through her.

When she'd taken off the shirt, she stood frozen for a moment as the dry breeze found the six-inch welts crisscrossing her back. She removed her boots and denims and the long, men's underwear clinging to her muscular thighs and flaring hips, and padded barefoot into the stream, touching her fingers to the welts on her bottom. They'd scabbed nicely and might not even leave scars.

Flagg, after she found him, should be so lucky.

She walked upstream until she found a wide flat pool. She sat down in the pool, in the soft, cool sand, rested on her arms, and threw her head back, arching her back and pushing her breasts up proudly. She grinned when she thought of the men staring down from a nearby scarp, an evil, girlish titter escaping her lips.

Slowly, she lowered her back into the water. A delicious chill coursed through her as the hard, crusted cuts sucked in the moisture from the stream.

She lifted her hands, cupping water onto her thighs, hips, and belly. She dippered several handfuls onto her breasts, then massaged the water around on them, chuckling again when she thought of the men watching from above.

They probably had at least one spyglass between them. Saradee's mouth opened wide as she laughed. They were getting one hell of an eyeful.

"Come and get it, boys . . ."

She got up slowly, catlike, and stretched. Then she stood, walked slowly back along the stream, lifting each foot with a dancer's flourish, and dried off with her saddle blanket, dressed, and fed more wood to the fire. When the flames were burning well, crackling as they fed on the dry mesquite she'd gathered from the other side of the stream, she set coffee to boil. That was about all she had in the way of food, for she'd left Cartridge Springs in such an ill temper that she'd forgotten to put on trail supplies.

She pulled her cast-iron skillet out of her saddlebag, though, and greased it from a small tub of bacon fat. Her keen ears—keen as any Indian's—had already picked up the slow clomp of oncoming riders.

A half hour later, she spread her saddle blanket beside the fire. She set the coffee to one side of the highest flames and sat down on the blanket. She leaned back against a rock, tipped her hat brim low, crossed her arms on her breasts, and closed her eyes.

Half-dozing, she smiled to herself, listening to the sounds of boots softly crunching gravel before her and to her right. The sounds got louder, stopped. A gun hammer clicked back.

"Hello, little miss."

Saradee jerked her head up with a start, snapping her eyes wide with feigned surprise. "Oh!"

Two of the ragtag trail riders stood ten feet on the other side of the fire. The other two stood to her left. Three aimed pistols at her. The red-headed kid in the stovepipe hat aimed an old trapdoor rifle. His broad grin showed two rows of tobacco-brown teeth tipped like fenceposts after a Plains twister had gone through farm country.

"Now, now, nothin' to be afraid of," he said. "Long as you cooperate."

All four stood staring at her, their grins not reaching their eyes. Their dust-streaked faces were flushed with lust.

The tall, one-eyed gent glanced at the shell belt wrapped around the two pistols to Saradee's right. "Nice and easy, toss those hoglegs over here, by my feet." He stared down his pistol barrel at her warningly. "Nice and slow."

Making her hands shake a little, Saradee slipped each pistol from its holster in turn, tossing it into the sand on the other side of the fire.

"Ah, Jesus," she said, her fear-sharp eyes darting from one gun-wielding hard case to the other. "You aren't *all* gonna take me at *once*, are you?"

The redhead chuckled through his teeth, spit bubbles popping along his gums.

Saradee shuddered, made her voice thin. "I'll cooperate if you will. Just one at a time. And you gotta promise not to kill me, and to leave a little meat when you're through."

The one-eyed man spat into the fire. He kept his glistening eye on Saradee as he strode toward her. "Sure, we'll leave a little meat."

"Hey," said the man with the drooping mustaches, grabbing his arm. "What makes you think you can go first?"

"Yeah," growled the redhead as he and the man with the muttonchops and washed-out eyes both turned toward the one-eyed gent.

It was the break Saradee had been banking on.

She lifted her right thigh, flipped up the saddle blanket, and plucked her spare Colt off the ground. Raising it, she clicked the hammer back, aimed at the one-eyed gent, and fired. The man's eye disappeared, vaporized as the bullet smashed through it and out the back of his head, throwing him straight back into the brush with nary a shriek.

"Hey!" barked the man with the muttonchops, swinging toward Saradee.

Quickly but calmly, Saradee shuttled the Colt toward him, thumbing back the hammer, and fired. He hadn't hit the ground, triggering his own pistol into the fire, before Saradee had drilled a slug through the chest of the man with the muttonchop whiskers.

The three men dropped like cans off fence posts.

As her third shot still echoed, out of the corner of her eye Saradee saw the redhead jerk back, shouting and raising his rifle. She hadn't yet recocked the Colt. Knowing he had the drop on her, Saradee threw herself forward and to the left. As she rolled off her left shoulder, the redhead's rifle barked, the slug slamming the rock where she'd been sitting an eye wink before.

Saradee came up off the shoulder, Colt cocked and extended, and fired.

"Ach!" cried the redhead, his right shoulder jerking back. He dropped the rifle and grabbed his upper right chest, bending at the waist and slitting his eyes. *"Bitch!"*

"That any way to talk to a helpless girl travelin' alone?" Saradee gained both knees, aimed the Colt, and fired. As she'd tripped the trigger, an ember in the fire had popped, and she'd jerked the slug slightly wide.

"Unh!" the redhead cried, as his right arm flapped out away from his body, the bullet searing his bicep and spraying blood. "Copper-riveted *whore*!"

He whipped away, fell to a knee, pushed up, and began running, tracing a jerky course through the darkening sage toward the horse trail.

Saradee knit her brows.

"Goddamnit."

She rose to her feet with a sigh. As the redhead's shrieks faded with distance, she stepped out away from the fire, stopped, spread her feet, aimed the Colt straight out before her, squinted down the barrel, and fired.

The redhead's head snapped forward. He ran a few more yards, all four limbs flopping crazily, then hit the ground on his chest and slid another ten feet before coming to rest against a Joshua tree.

Through the wafting powder smoke, Saradee looked around at the three ragtag hard cases nearest the fire. All appeared quite dead. She holstered her Colt, dragged them far enough away from her camp that she wouldn't trip over them during the night, then strolled off in search of their horses.

A half hour later, she sat by the fire, biscuits browning in her greased pan, side pork frying in another. She sipped her coffee seasoned with the hard cases' whiskey, and counted the money from their saddlebags.

"Three thousand, four hundred and thirty-six dollars," she said when she was shoving the greenbacks back in the pouch. "Not bad for a no-account girl from the Panhandle."

18.

CAGED

IN the small but comfortable casa she shared with Dona Carmelita Sandoval, Juliana lifted her head from her straw sleeping pallet and pricked her ears, listening.

Low snores drifted from behind the woven curtain separating the girl's room from Carmelita's. Satisfied the old woman was sound asleep, Juliana flung her blankets aside, rose, lifted her nightdress over her head, and tossed it onto a dresser.

She'd gone to bed several hours ago, but had only dozed as she waited for the chill night to settle over the canyon and for Carmelita to drift into deep sleep. Now, the night had settled, so cold that goose bumps rose on Juliana's arms as she padded about the earthen-floored room, blindly gathering her clothes in the stygian darkness, and dressing.

When she'd donned heavy underclothes, a simple gray dress, a poncho, and sandals, she slipped out of her room and into the casa's small kitchen area. Moving toward the beehive fireplace still emanating heat and a dull, orange glow, she kicked a chair. The leg scraped the floor with a low bark.

Juliana sucked a breath and lifted her head, tensing and listening. Carmelita's snores had ceased. Juliana waited, her hands squeezing the chair back. She'd begun stepping backward, intending to return to her room, when the old woman smacked her lips, sighed, and resumed snoring once more.

Juliana released a heavy breath and moved toward a shelf to the right of the fireplace. Rising up on her toes, she slid a tea can and several jars aside and felt around until her hand found what she was looking for. She pulled out the old, heavy pistol Carmelita had found in one of the shacks the miners had abandoned when the gold had played out.

Juliana had never fired the gun. She didn't even know if it was loaded. Carmelita kept it around to ward off unwanted callers for Juliana, so it must have had bullets in it.

The gun repelled her, and she didn't look at it too closely, but she slid it into the poncho's deep front pocket, over her belly, then stepped lightly through the casa's main living area to the front door.

She took one last look behind her, only the dim umber glow showing at the back of the house, then opened the timbered door, stepped outside, and latched the door softly behind her. She shoved her hands into the openings on each side of the poncho's single pocket. Clasping the gun, she hunched her shoulders against the cold and began moving quickly across the yard and into the night.

When she arrived at the cobbled main street, she crouched behind a wheelless wagon, staring westward toward the saloon. To the left, the small, stone jailhouse hunched between an abandoned blacksmith shop and a harness maker's. A dim light shone in the two barred windows facing the main street. A man sat under the brush arbor, in a chair tipped back against the front wall—a hatted silhouette against the white stone, a rifle resting across his lap.

Juliana lightly tapped her fingers against the wagon's rotting sideboards as she considered the situation. If she tried to cross the street here, the deputy would no doubt see her.

Finally, she rose, turned into an alley, crossed the main street a hundred yards east of the jailhouse, and approached the jailhouse from the alley behind it.

To her left, a stand of tall cottonwoods tossed their large leaves in the breeze. Starlight played on the stream curving behind the trees, with its low, tinny murmur. The sound of the water should cover any sounds she herself might make.

Stepping slowly across the shale and through the spindly shrubs that had grown up around the jailhouse, she pressed her hands to the cold stones of the rear wall. Four barred windows were small, rectangular shapes in the wall above her, nearly six feet off the ground. She reached up, grabbed the ledge of the first window, rose up on the tips of her toes, and edged a look into the cell.

The cell itself was dark, but she could see that it was empty, its door hanging halfway open. Beyond the cell and to the left was a desk on which a lamp burned low. Sitting at the desk, his feet crossed on the desk top, sat one of the deputies. He leaned back in a swivel chair, hands crossed behind his head. Soft snores rose.

She turned her head to look into the next cell, but it was too dark to see anything from this angle. She removed her hands from the ledge and looked warily around, hearing only the leaves and the stream. She moved to the next window, rose up again on her tiptoes, and peered inside.

At the same time that she saw a silhouetted face staring back at her, a familiar, hushed voice said her name. She jerked back with a start, heart pounding. She looked again at the window. Gideon stared back at her through the bars—a gaunt, haunted figure in the darkness.

"Gideon," she whispered, moving back to the wall, placing her hands on the crumbling ledge grainy with dust and old pigeon droppings.

"Go home, Juliana."

She moved her face up close to his.

His eyes had receded within their dark sockets, and the

leathery skin had tightened across his cheekbones. He seemed depleted, somehow. Sapped of energy and life. Seeing him there, like a caged animal, wrenched her heart, and a sudden sob escaped her lips.

Tears dribbled down her cheeks.

"Gideon, I—"

He closed his hand around hers on one of the bars. "It isn't safe here. If you want to help me, you'll go home and stay there till these men are gone."

"I *love* you, Gideon. I want us to be together always. What I've done haunts me . . . how I led them right to you!"

"They would've gotten me, anyway."

"You would've gotten them."

"You want to be married to a killer?"

She lifted her head to answer, but he cut her off.

"You're good and sweet and honorable, Juliana. Go home and forget me. Wait for the right man. Raise a big family, and shower your love all over them. You've got a lot of it to shower, Juliana. *Love* your family. Hold them close every day, because you never know . . ."

Hawk let the sentence die on his lips. He lowered his eyes, removed his hand from hers. He stepped back, kept his voice just above a whisper. "Go home."

A sleep-thick voice grumbled behind him. "Hey, who you talkin' to over there?"

Hawk turned his head sharply, heart thudding. Beyond the dark cell, kicked back in the chair, Franco Villard had turned his head to regard Hawk incredulously.

"Go back to sleep," Hawk told him. "I was just watching the star—"

Beyond the window, Juliana gave a clipped scream. Hawk whipped his head around to see a tall, duster-clad figure holding her hands. Starlight winked off the object in her right hand and off the badge pinned to the deputy's duster lapel. J.C. Garth's voice was a chuckling reprimand. "What the hell you think you're doin' out here, sweetheart?"

Hawk grabbed the bars. "Let her go!"

Behind him, Villard shouted, "What the hell's goin' on out there?"

Hawk hardly heard him. He was watching Juliana struggle with the deputy. Garth dodged a kick and wrenched Juliana's right hand behind her back. She yowled as her head jerked back, hair flying.

"No!"

There was the solid, metallic thud of a heavy gun hitting the ground.

Both Garth and Juliana froze, staring down at the old-model Colt in the dust. Garth's head snapped up and he took one long stride toward Juliana, swinging his right hand back to his left shoulder. "You little *bitch*!"

He brought the open hand forward, the knuckles connecting solidly with Juliana's right cheek. She gave a cry as she whipped around and fell against the stone wall with a smack.

"Garth!" Hawk barked, squeezing the bars, half-hearing the jailhouse's front door slam and boots pounding the stoop. Running footsteps sounded on the west side of the jail, and then Villard ran around the corner, hatless, breathing hard.

"What the hell's—?"

Garth reached down for the gun. He turned it in his hands, studying it. "Little bitch brought our friend a weapon. Here."

He tossed the revolver to Villard, who caught it, gave it a quick study, then lowered it, dropping his gaze to the girl. Hawk could see only Juliana's legs beneath the window and to the right. Her skirts had come up, revealing nearly all of one finely turned thigh. She'd lost her sandals, and her bare feet pushed at the dirt and rocks beneath her, seeking purchase.

The cool night air was tinged with the smell of whiskey. The deputies had been sharing a bottle for the past two hours. Pulse throbbing in his temples, Hawk renewed his grip on the bars and shuttled his gaze between the two men staring silently down at Juliana. Garth's hand was fisted, and his chest rose and fell heavily.

"Let her go, boys. She meant no harm."

Silence. The men's breath mixed with the rasping of the cottonwood leaves barely audible above the stream's trickle over the rocks behind them.

Villard gave his head a hard shake, ran his hand through his curly red hair. "A fine-lookin' girl you got here, Hawk. Yessir. Fine piece of work."

Garth swallowed. "Girls just throw themselves at a *hero*, don't they?"

Hawk's voice was low and pitched with menace. "Let her go."

"Why should we?" said Villard. "She's trash mixin' with outlaw trash and callin' him a damn hero."

"You're lawmen."

Villard laughed. "That's real funny, comin' from you, Hawk."

Juliana dug her heels into the sand, pushed herself to her feet, and lunged toward the side of the jailhouse. Villard grabbed her poncho and threw her down.

She sat up, tossing her hair from her eyes and turning to Hawk. "Gideon!"

Garth moved toward her, heavy-footed, swaying drunkenly. Hawk warned through gritted teeth, spittle spraying from his lips, "You touch her, I'll kill you both."

Garth spat. "Fuckin' bitch. Tryin' to give him a gun . . . what? . . . so's he can shoot us? You're nothin' but a whore! *His* whore. Now you're gonna be *my* whore."

He grabbed her arm, jerked her to her feet.

Juliana whipped her head again to Hawk, beseeching with her eyes. "No!"

Villard lunged toward her. "Shut up, whore!" He slapped her hard across the face. She twisted around and fell in a heap, sobbing. "Please, no!"

Staring through the window, Hawk clutched the bars as if to bend them with his fists. There was no give at all. He pulled and jerked till his knuckles felt as though they'd pop through his skin, veins bulging in his forehead. Outside, Villard grabbed Juliana's arm and jerked her up.

"No!" She lunged at him, fists flying.

Villard laughed and ducked, turned her around, grabbed her from behind, and nuzzled her neck. She turned, rammed a knee into his groin. As Villard bent over his bruised oysters, cursing, Garth staggered toward her and raised his fist.

"Garth!" Hawk raged.

At the same time, Garth shouted, "Whore!" and slammed his fist against Juliana's right cheek. The girl flew like a rag doll, hitting the ground in a heap. She lay writhing and groaning.

Rage burning through him like fire-tipped arrows, Hawk wheeled and lunged at the door. He shook the bars, rattling the lock. The bolt held fast.

"Goddamnit!"

He wheeled again to the window. Garth and Villard were dragging Juliana off toward the cottonwoods, the girl a slumped figure between them, her legs dragging along the ground.

"Villard!"

The deputy glanced behind him, starlight making his sweaty face glisten. "Sit tight, Hawk. Take a load off. We'll be back shortly."

Both deputies chuckled as they disappeared into the darkness of the cottonwoods.

Gripping the bars in both fists, Hawk closed his eyes and gritted his teeth. In the distance, just above the stream's gurgle, he heard the men laughing, heard the sound of clothes tearing, Juliana whimpering and pleading. Hawk shoved the sounds aside, replaced them with images of both deputies lying dead upon the rocks, their heads bashed in with stones.

Juliana's cry rose shrilly, muffled by the stream and the men's laughter. "No . . . no . . . please . . ."

Hawk's eyes flickered. He squeezed them shut, clamped his jaws till their hinges dimpled, the muscles in his crimson cheeks fairly leaping out from beneath the skin.

When he'd been standing there at the barred window for what seemed like hours but was probably only a few minutes, a loud smack jerked his eyes open. It sounded like a stout branch smashed against a boulder. A man yowled.

Another voice. "Hey . . . what do you? . . ."

A choking, gurgling sound, like that from a man with his throat cut.

Hawk spied movement back in the trees—two shadows running toward him, one before the other. The first ran, faltering, with both hands clutched to his throat, blood glistening in the starlight. As his gait lurched and he dropped to his knees, the second silhouette—short, and wearing a low-crowned sombrero—lifted a heavy plank above his head and slammed it down with a resolute, cracking thud against the head of the first.

The first man arched his back, and he sat for several seconds, as if staring skyward and praying. Then he sagged to his side, both hands coming away from his throat.

The sombrero-clad shadow tossed the plank into the brush and walked toward Hawk. As he drew closer, the stooped, bandy-legged figure of Palomar Rojas took shape in the darkness.

"Ayee!" the old man wheezed, wincing and holding one arm taut against his side. "That hurt me more than him, I think."

19.

FLIGHT

HAWK followed the old man around the corner of the jailhouse with his eyes, then wheeled and crossed to the cell door. He stood there, brows furrowed, as Palomar Rojas opened the building's main door, casting a wary glance toward the saloon a block away.

Inside the office, he closed the door and hurried to the desk, wincing and holding his right elbow tight to his ribs.

"The key's in the bottom drawer," Hawk said. "You kill him?"

Rojas spread his swollen, cracked lips in a grin. "Oh, yes." Key in hand, the old bandito ambled over to the cell and shoved the key in the lock. When he flung the door open, Hawk bolted out, grabbed his gun belt from a wall peg, wrapped it around his waist, then picked up one of the two Winchesters leaning against the wall near the desk.

He opened the breech, made sure it was loaded, then ran to the front door.

He cracked the door, peered both ways along the street, then stepped slowly onto the boardwalk. Holding the rifle straight up and down before him, he sidestepped to the

building's east side, then turned and lit off toward the
stream. He could hear Rojas limping along behind him.

Hawk jogged through the brush around the cottonwoods, pausing to glance down at J.C. Garth lying on his
back, head turned to one side, the wide gash in his neck
stretching from ear to ear. The deputy's lips were pulled
back, showing the tips of his uneven teeth. Several streams
of blood trailed down from his smashed skull, disappearing in his beard.

Resisting the urge to bury a boot toe in the deputy's
ribs, Hawk continued forward twenty feet, where the
stocky figure of Leo Baskin crouched over Juliana,
smoothing her hair back from her face. The girl lay with
her head resting on a balled-up duck coat. Her torn blouse
was spread blanketlike across her chest. Her skirt was
twisted about her thighs.

Hawk crouched beside Baskin, his eyes on the girl.

Baskin growled, "Me and the old bandit had come to
spring you, when we saw those two with the girl."

"Is she? . . ."

"She's alive. Must've hit her head on a sharp rock. I felt
some blood."

Hawk followed Baskin's gaze into the brush beyond
Juliana. Franco Villard lay on his side, a wide knife gash
laying open his neck, the thick, pooling blood glistening in
the starlight. His lips were drawn back from his mouth in
a horrified death grin.

Holding a rifle across his thighs, Baskin turned to
Hawk. "Your horse is saddled and tied yonder. Best get a
move on."

Hawk frowned at him, his brain freezing up, unable to
make a decision.

"I'll take the girl home," Baskin said. "Carmelita'll take
care of her."

Boots crunched brush behind Hawk. He turned to see
Rojas ambling toward him. "You must go now, before the
others find your cell empty."

Hawk reached down and pulled the coat up closer to

Juliana's chin. She lay still but for muscles twitching in her cheeks. "I can't leave her."

"You must!" Rojas hissed.

Hawk dropped to both knees, snaking his arms beneath the girl's knees and neck. "I'm gonna take her home."

Rojas laid into him with a long string of exclamatory Spanish, which he cut off suddenly himself. He turned his head sharply to one side. At the same time, Hawk froze with the girl in his arms, her legs dangling.

Enraged voices rose inside the jailhouse, echoing dully.

"Shit!" Rojas spat. "Goddamn, what I tell you, gringo fool?"

An angry shout rose behind them. "Check around back!"

With Juliana in his arms, moaning softly, Hawk stood and turned to Rojas and Baskin. "You two, vamoose."

Both men shuttled quick, nervous glances between the jailhouse and Hawk.

"Now!" Hawk barked. *"Move!"*

As Baskin and Rojas scrambled off through the trees, angling southwest along the stream, Hawk headed straight east to where his horse stood tied to a big cottonwood. He couldn't leave the girl now. She'd slow him up, and she'd be better off with Carmelita, but he had no choice but to take her.

When he'd set her on his saddle, he snapped the reins free of the cottonwood branch and climbed up behind her. Several deputies were scrambling around the jailhouse now, jostling shadows against the pale bulk of the building. He could hear Press Miller cursing tightly as boots tapped a staccato rhythm beneath the stream's constant rush.

Hawk neck-reined the horse eastward and was about to press his knees to the mount's ribs when a rifle popped and several small branches snapped to his right before the slug spanged loudly off a rock several yards beyond. In his arms, Juliana gave a soft, startled cry, tensing.

"There!" a deputy shouted.

Facing straight ahead, Hawk rammed his heels against the grulla's flanks. "Hee-yaa!"

Another rifle snap. Then another, the slugs pounding the rocks and brush as the grulla leapt off its back hooves and bounded straight east through the trees.

When the grulla had galloped thirty yards, Hawk turned right and splashed into the stream. He galloped the horse back the way he'd come, the hooves clacking off stones and splashing water, enraged voices rising on the stream bank to his right.

The deputies were taken aback by the maneuver, however, and only a few shots came close. The grulla whinnied as the slugs spanged off rocks or plunked into the water. In a minute, Hawk was a hundred yards beyond the lawmen, tracing a gradual curve toward the northeast as the deputies triggered a couple of halfhearted shots behind.

Beyond the village, he turned the horse onto the narrow, seldom-used western trail ribboning into the high, rough country beyond the old mine and stamping mill and smelter. He pushed the grulla as hard as he could on the treacherous trail in the darkness, watching with his mind's eye as the four remaining deputies scrambled to the livery barn, saddled their horses, and headed straight west of town. Miller would take the lead, shouting orders.

They didn't know the country out here, but it wouldn't take them long to realize there was only one trail into the badlands, which were too rugged and dry for even Apaches. Only one trail twisting through the high-walled canyons and cactus-studded gorges—a veritable dinosaur's mouth of rifted earth and mountains and mesas rising from an ancient seabed, dry for countless ages.

A perfect place for a man to hide. If he knew where to find the single water hole that existed and if that water hole wasn't dry, as it was for most of the year.

If so, well then, the joke would be on Hawk and the girl.

Juliana slumped against him as the grulla made its way along the uneven path, climbing into cedars and junipers and dropping into gorges and clay-bottom washes where

only rocks and boulders grew, with occasional tufts of
Spanish bayonet or low, spindly catclaw.

When he'd ridden for nearly an hour, he paused beneath
a lip of overhanging rock and set his hand on Juliana's
right shoulder. He whispered her name, then knew a moment's trepidation when she lay deathlike against him,
silent.

"Juliana?" he repeated, louder.

Her head moved slightly, sliding across his chest, and a
low groan escaped her. It didn't make sense that she wasn't
waking up by now. She must've been hurt worse than he'd
thought, and this ride wasn't doing her any good at all.

Hawk expelled a frustrated breath but kept his hand on
her shoulder as, hearing something, he canted his head to
listen.

Behind rose the faint click and clatter of shod hooves.
Occasional voices lifted, the lawmen no doubt arguing,
blaming each other for their predicament. Hawk couldn't
help smiling as he wondered if someone had told Flagg
about the empty jail cell, the two dead deputies. If he and
Juliana made it back to Bedlam alive, he owed Baskin
and that old reprobate, Rojas, a case of the best brandy and
some good smoking tobacco.

He nudged the grulla with his spurs, riding on.

He stopped twice to offer Juliana water from the canteen, but she only shook her head and fell back against his
chest, barely opening her eyes.

Concern for the girl eating at him, he continued riding,
twisting through the badlands as the sun slowly rose, gray
light seeming to emanate from the mountains and mesas
and rocky turrets themselves before a burst of rose appeared over Hawk's left shoulder. The sun vaulted over the
eastern ridges, scattering shadows until the vast, moonlike
terrain stood out sharply on all sides, capped with a dry,
cobalt sky.

Hawk turned around a tall, arrow-shaped scarp and
reined the grulla to a halt.

A rock wall loomed before him, connecting the sheer

walls on both sides. He'd found the box canyon he was looking for.

Turning toward the north, he raised his gaze up along the shelving ridge thrusting giant spires and arches over the canyon. The spring should be up there, behind that sandstone block with what looked like three chimneys pointing skyward.

Hawk dismounted and led the horse up the ridge, moving slowly across three treacherous talus slides.

Twenty minutes later, he halted the horse on the far side of the sandstone block. Between the block and the ridge wall was a V-shaped trough of rocks around which some spindly junipers and Mormon tea grew. There was plenty of animal scat and tracks around the trough. In the trough itself were several inches of black, scummy water.

Up the slope beyond the spring was a shady spot amongst boulders. Hawk dropped the grulla's reins, then reached up and eased Juliana into his arms. He didn't like it that she barely stirred as he pulled her out of the saddle, then hung limp in his arms as he carried her up the slope and eased her down in the shade amongst the rocks.

She groaned and turned her head from side to side, her thick hair like a pillow beneath her. Hawk frowned and ran his right hand through her hair, crusty with dried blood. Her eyes opened, and they took a while to focus.

"Where are we?" she asked thinly.

Hawk kept his voice quiet, calm. "I had to get you out of town."

"I caused more trouble." She winced and rolled her eyes to one side, as if to indicate from where the pain came. "What happened?"

Hawk wasn't sure what to say. If she didn't remember what had happened behind the jailhouse, he wasn't going to tell her. He put a finger to her lips, cracked a wan smile. "You rest. Can you drink some water?"

"Maybe a little."

He rose and started toward his horse.

"Gideon?"

Hawk turned back to her.

She stared up at him, brown eyes crinkled at the corners from pain. Trail dust streaked her face. "I love you."

Hawk dropped to one knee. He placed a hand along her cheek, ran his thumb across her chin, then leaned over her, pressed his lips to hers. The coolness of her lips made his stomach tighten. He stared into her eyes, and she quirked a half smile, a dim, copper light dancing far back in her eyes.

"I'll be right back."

He stood, walked over to the grulla, and grabbed the canteen from around the saddle horn. The canteen had been full when he'd left Bedlam, but he'd given half to the grulla. What was left was no doubt warm. He squatted beside the spring, smoothed the surface scum away from the black pool, and submerged the canteen. Water gurgled through the spout, and the flask grew heavy.

Lifting it from the pool, Hawk took a drink to make sure it tasted fresh, then walked back to Juliana.

"It isn't cold," he said, removing the cork and dropping to one knee beside her. "But it isn't half bad for—"

He froze with the canteen partly lowered to her lips. Her eyes stared right through him, lips parted slightly, her chest still.

Hawk's voice quivered. "Juliana?"

He touched her shoulder. There was no reaction. He set down the canteen and lowered his right ear to her lips. No rustle of breath. His chest grew heavy and a knot grew in his throat as he set his hand upon her bosom, feeling no heartbeat.

His own heart raced for a time, and then it slowed gradually. Tears dribbled down his cheeks, though his eyes remained hard.

Finally, he leaned down, kissed her lips, then lifted her hand and kissed the smooth flesh above the knuckles.

Behind his eyes, he saw Jubal drop from the wind-battered cottonwood on the rain-swept hill. He watched Linda's lithe body, hanging slack from the tree in their backyard, turn gently in the breeze, the morning light turning her blond hair to gold.

Hawk flinched as if from a sharp slap, then ran his fingers lightly over Juliana's face, closing her eyes. He crossed her hands on her chest, squeezed them gently, then rose with a low, involuntary groan that welled up from deep inside.

Down canyon, horse hooves thumped and clattered. He turned to see a thin veil of dust rising from the eastern canyon floor.

Hawk glanced once more at Juliana, then turned, walked back to the grulla, slid the Winchester from the saddle boot, and levered a shell into the breach.

20.

SARADEE'S REVENGE

PALOMAR Rojas stood outside Green's saloon's batwing doors, puffing a stubby, black cheroot as he stared westward.

At high noon, the light fell brassily over Bedlam, making the abandoned hovels lining the street look even more godforsaken than usual. A dust devil danced over the dry stone fountain in the middle of the trash-littered square and fizzled. The straw, chicken feathers, and flecks of dried goat dung settled over the boardwalk in front of what once had been a barbershop.

Behind Rojas, Leo Baskin's boots pounded down the stairs at the back of the saloon. The barman, who had made countless trips to Flagg's room with whiskey, fresh bandages, or tobacco, stopped at the bottom landing. His broken nose gave his voice a nasal quality.

"When you suppose that son of a bitch is gonna give up the ghost?"

Rojas glanced into the saloon's perpetually murky shadows. He swept a fly from his face and puffed, stretching his lips back from the wet cheroot in his teeth. "Maybe I should encourage him a little, huh?"

"Better wait," Baskin said, heading for the bar with one of the several empty whiskey bottles he'd removed from Flagg's room. He tossed the bottle into a barrel with a loud, glassy clatter. "We'll see if those deputies return for him. If not, I'm not gonna keep servin' him whiskey and tendin' his wounds. Bastard's gonna drink himself to death sooner or later, anyway, and I got a sneakin' suspicion no one'd miss him."

Rojas was staring west again, sucking and puffing the cigar. "They will not return. Hawk will return in another day, maybe two." He smiled. "The buzzards and the wolves will pick and scatter the deputies' bones . . . and it will be as if they had never lived." He smiled, impressed by his melodrama.

"But am I gonna have any whiskey left?" Baskin said, slamming a fresh bottle on the bar top. "There's the question I want answered."

"Piss in an empty bottle," Rojas advised. "He won't know the difference."

"I'm just about out of bandage cloth, too."

Rojas snorted. "You worry too much, Leo." He turned and started back into the saloon, but stopped when a dog yipped behind him and a horse whinnied shrilly.

"Who the hell's that dog after now?" growled Baskin from behind the bar.

About fifty yards from Rojas, a horse and rider were being harassed by the little three-legged cur that hung around Miguel Taibo's goat pens. The dog yipped at the big palomino's left rear hock as the horse reared slightly and swung its rump toward the opposite side of the street.

The girl astride the horse—a lean, high-breasted blonde, dressed in men's trail garb but most definitely a senorita to make a man's blood roil—drew one of the two pistols thonged low on her hips. Holding the reins taut in her left hand, she snapped off two shots with her right.

The slugs blew up grit and cobble shards around the little dog, which screeched, wheeled on its sole rear leg, and disappeared between the hovels on the street's south side.

The blonde stared after the dog. She took a moment to replace the two spent shells in the Colt's cylinder, then, looking around cautiously and readjusting the red velvet pillow padding her saddle, swung the horse back into the street and nudged it forward. When she spied Rojas standing on the saloon's porch, she turned the palomino toward the saloon. The magnificent horse approached slowly, hanging its head and breathing hard, its cream-bronze coat glistening with sweat.

The girl pulled up to the hitch rack and stopped. A smear of dirt on her right cheek somehow pointed up the beauty of her smooth-skinned, suntanned, heart-shaped face. "If that's your dog, I wasn't tryin' to kill him, just trim his tail a little."

Rojas wasn't sure which impressed him more, the high-busted blonde in the beaded vest over a blue-checked shirt, or the broad-chested horse she straddled. Baskin had walked up to flank him on the other side of the door. "I wish someone would trim more than his tail," the barman said.

"Bad luck to shoot a three-legged dog." The girl glanced around the street, then shuttled her blue eyes back to the old bandito. "Where's the posse?"

Rojas had removed the cheroot from his teeth. Now he replaced it and, holding it between his lips with a gnarled, brown hand, gave it a few pensive puffs as he studied her. "What posse might you be talking about, senorita?"

"The posse of seven that came here after Hawk." She shifted her weight on the pillow, wincing slightly, then leaned forward and rested her arm on the saddle horn. "I'm guessing the coyotes are wrestling over their bones up in the mountains by now, but I'd be particularly interested in the fate of their leader, one D.W. Flagg. Might even be worth a few dollars to you."

Rojas and Baskin shared a glance, the barman's lips stretching a taut smile beneath his swollen, purple nose and bloodshot eyes. "How many's a few?"

"Well, let's see now." The blonde hipped around in her

saddle, reached into a saddlebag, and produced a small bundle of tightly wrapped greenbacks. One-handed, she riffled the bills, her blue eyes crossing slightly as she inspected them, then tossed the bundle onto the boardwalk. They hit the boards with a soft thump.

Baskin pushed through the batwings and crouched to scoop the money off the porch's scarred floor. He ran a finger over one end, riffling the bills, then turned to Rojas. "Jesus Christ, there's a hundred dollars here!"

Rojas took another slow puff from his cigar, his brown eyes flashing whimsically. "Miss, uh . . ."

"Jones."

"Miss Jones, perhaps you should alight and allow Senor Baskin to buy you a drink?"

She raked her eyes across both men, narrowing her eyes with cunning and swinging her right leg over the palomino's rump. "Perhaps."

When she'd looped her reins over the hitch rack and mounted the porch, she stopped before Rojas, plucked the cheroot from between his lips, stuck it between her own, and puffed. She rolled the cigar to one corner of her mouth, giving the old bandito a level stare.

"Keep in mind, I only drink with hombres who make it worth my time."

Rojas watched her take several puffs off his cigar, and swallowed, feeling his face warm and his heart speed up as her lips opened and closed around the thick, black cylinder.

She glanced at Baskin. "And I certainly wouldn't want to waste time on men who'd take advantage of my"—she nibbled the cigar—"innocence."

Baskin winced as if from a physical pain, and glanced at the two well-oiled, pearl-gripped Colts thonged low on her hips. "Miss Jones, I'd never think of it. And I can assure you Senor Rojas wouldn't, either."

"*Sí,*" rasped the old bandit.

"Well," said Saradee, removing the cigar from her lips and poking it back into Rojas's mouth, "let's see about that drink, then."

She followed Baskin into the empty, dark saloon. She bellied up to the bar as Baskin walked around behind it and Rojas sat tenderly down at a table near the door and slapped a greasy card deck onto the table's scarred surface.

"Just got a fresh bottle out for the gent upstairs," Baskin said. "He won't mind if you have a shot or two from it. Probably won't know the difference."

As Baskin splashed whiskey into the shot glass before Saradee, Rojas chuckled behind her, shuffling his cards. Saradee picked up the filmy glass in her gloved hand, studied the whiskey, then threw it back.

Above her head, a familiar voice shouted, "Goddamnit, Baskin, if you don't hurry up with that bottle I'm gonna start shooting through the floor!"

Saradee froze with her head tilted back, the shot glass still pressed to her lips. She stared at the glass's thick bottom, a single bead of whiskey dribbling over her lower lip and into her mouth, burning like pepper. Slowly, she lowered the glass and set it on the bar top without a sound.

Baskin smiled. "His men rode out west after Hawk. Me and Rojas don't think they'll be back." He splashed another shot into Saradee's glass and corked the bottle. "Perhaps you'd like to deliver this to my guest upstairs?"

Saradee's face was hot. She closed her fingers around the glass, squeezed it, raised it to her lips, and threw it back. She set the glass down and smacked her lips.

"Perhaps."

She shook her hair off her shoulders, picked up the bottle, and glanced at Rojas. He held his cards in his hands, smiling at her around his dead cigar, little longer than a sewing thimble.

Holding the bottle by the neck, Saradee removed a leather quirt from a pocket of the beaded vest she'd pulled off the tall, one-eyed outlaw she'd ventilated, then sauntered over to the stairs and began climbing one step at a time.

"Room four," Baskin said.

"Obliged."

She gained the top of the stairs and strode to room four. Turning the knob, she nudged the door wide.

Flagg sat on the far side of the room in a Windsor chair angled so that he could see westward down the village's main street. His boots were crossed on the window sill. The room smelled like piss, shit, overripe bandages, and tobacco.

On the other side of a heavy smoke cloud, Flagg turned his haggard, gray-bearded face toward Saradee. His skin looked like chalk, and his gray eyes were red-rimmed above sagging, lead-colored pouches. Both arms were suspended in slings and wrapped in bloody bandages. He held a thin cigar between the first two fingers of his right hand.

Flagg scowled at Saradee, giving her a long once-over before his eyes suddenly darkened with recognition, and he stiffened in his chair.

"Hello, Marshal." Saradee grinned and raised the bottle, indicating his bloody arms. "I see you found Hawk."

Flagg grunted and winced as he dropped his right hand toward the pistol on his thigh. He cursed as he realized he couldn't lower his hand with the sling around it. Trying another tactic, he began slowly backing the arm out of the sling, groaning and panting like a whipped dog.

Saradee laughed, set the bottle on a washstand, and strode casually toward him. He looked up at her, eyes widening as, just before he got his hand out of the sling, she reached down and slipped the gun from his holster. He clawed at it, missing by several inches.

Saradee flipped the gun, caught it by the barrel, then smashed the butt over the bloody bandage on his arm.

"Ahhh!"

Flagg sagged over in the chair, holding the quivering arm taut to his side, his face turning even whiter than before. *"Bitch!"*

Again, Saradee slung the revolver's butt against the bloody bandage on Flagg's arm. He howled.

Saradee grabbed his chin, turned his face toward her, and stuck the barrel of Flagg's Remington in his mouth. He gagged and tried to pull away. She thumbed the hammer back and he froze, staring up at her along both sides of the revolver.

His eyes twitched as he awaited a bullet. The bandage on his right arm shone brightly with fresh blood.

"I'm calling a note due, Marshal Flagg. You're gonna climb onto the bed, and I'm going to tie you up like you did me." She ripped a sheet off the bed and held up the braided leather quirt. "Remember this?"

Flagg glowered at her, eyes rheumy from whiskey. Sweat streaked his face. His left eye twitched.

Saradee rammed the revolver's barrel deeper down his throat. Gagging, he nodded frantically.

"You're gonna stand up and pull your pants down for Saradee. Aren't you?"

Flagg just stared up at her through rheumy eyes, veins forking above his nose. As she adjusted her grip on the pistol and took up the trigger slack, he nodded frantically again.

Saradee removed the gun from his mouth, spittle stringing off the end of the barrel. He gagged for nearly a minute, tears washing down his cheeks. Saradee backed away from him, keeping the cocked revolver aimed at his face.

"I hope you have a thicker hide than I do," she said, rubbing her butt with her free hand.

"You can't do this to me, goddamnit," Flagg gasped. "I'm a United States marshal!" He canted his head toward the door. *"Baskin!"*

Saradee wagged the gun, ordering him up, then aimed the barrel at his face. Slowly, wincing as he pushed his elbows against the chair arms, Flagg gained his feet. He stood looking down at her, his pupils narrowing devilishly as though he were contemplating trying to grab the gun from her hand.

Taunting him, she wagged the revolver at his pants.

He looked at his black denims, as if surprised to see them on his legs, then looked again at Saradee. He opened his mouth to speak. She edged the gun higher, slitting one eye and tightening her jaws.

Again, he canted his head toward the door. "Baskin, get this crazy bitch out of my room!"

Saradee fired the Remy. Flagg winced and jerked his head back, then rolled his eyes to the right, as if trying to see the slight notch she'd carved in his ear. He shuttled his gaze back to her, wide eyes bright with horror.

Saradee cocked the revolver and canted the barrel toward his crotch. "Better get to work, or I'm gonna make Mrs. Flagg a very frustrated woman."

Flagg blinked and stretched his lips back from his teeth as a fine stream of blood dribbled down from his ear. "I'm gonna have my deputies hunt you down. There'll be nowhere you can hide. Nowhere!"

Staring at the pistol aimed at his crotch, he moved his hands to his waist, began unbuckling his pistol belt. When he'd dropped the belt and holster on the floor, he sat down on the bed, dropped his gaze to the floor. "Baskin, I'll have your head for this, you son of a bitch!"

Hearing only muffled chuckles below, he glanced again at Saradee, then unbuttoned his pants and began peeling them down to his boots, a slow, painful process with his bullet-shredded arms.

When he was naked from the waist down and his face was blotched with silent fury, he turned around and lay belly down on the bed, the springs squeaking under his weight. "You won't get away with it," he rasped. "You crazy bitch, I'll hunt you down, kill you like a rogue she-griz—"

"She-griz," Saradee chuckled, setting the pistol aside and picking up the sheet she'd torn from the bed. "I like that. That's kind of how I've always seen myself."

She tore four long strips from the sheet and tied Flagg's wrists and ankles to the bedposts. The marshal cursed her all the while, and cursed Baskin and Rojas downstairs, blood seeping out from under his bandages to soak the bed beneath his arms.

When she'd made sure that all the knots were tight, she grabbed her quirt off the washstand and stepped up to the bed, holding the quirt's braided leather shaft in one hand while running the other along the loop at the business end, the two long, horsehair whangs hanging off the loop like streamers.

"Where I come from, these are called rug beaters," Saradee said, slashing the loop through the air over Flagg's naked ass.

His bottom was rather broad for a man's, with patches of thin brown hair and several tender-looking saddle galls sprouting from the powder-white skin. "That's one tender ass you have there, Flagg. You need to stop spending so much time in the office."

Arms stretched above his head, Flagg turned an eye to her, his chalky, sweaty face mottled red. "I'm gonna hunt you down."

"You won't need to pull your shirt up," Saradee said, ignoring him and flicking the quirt through the air once more. It made a savage whistle. "Your ass is all *I* want."

As the last two words left her mouth, she slammed the quirt down resolutely upon Flagg's ass. Flagg made no sound, just lifted his head straight off the bed and pulled at the ties holding his wrists to the bedposts.

A dark-pink welt rose instantly across the middle of both buttocks.

"Doesn't feel very good, does it, Marshal?" She swung the quirt over her shoulder, the noose flopping against her back. She raised it high, slammed it down on Flagg's butt.

Again, Flagg lifted his head sharply, breathing through his nose and fisting his tied hands.

His voice was thin and shaky, just above a whisper. "Goddamn you. Goddamn you fucking cunt whore to hell!"

Crack!

"That one feel any better? No? How 'bout *that* one?"

Crack!

Flagg loosed a taut whimper. "I'm gonna . . . I'm gonna kill Baskin and Rojas. I'm gonna fucking *kill* 'em!"

When she'd flogged him five times and was finding her stride, Flagg kept his head raised above the bed, teeth gritted, eyes squeezed shut. He gave a little, coyotelike yodel now and then, but mostly he held his body taut and sucked air sharply through his nose.

After about ten minutes, his head sagged slowly down to the pillow, and his body fell slack. She laid into him for another couple of minutes, then, breathless and sweating, she stopped. Heart pounding, she stared down at Flagg's ass.

It was a mess of bloody stripes, the galls looking as though they'd exploded from the inside out. The quirt was bloody, too. She tossed it down on Flagg's back, ran her wrist across her mouth, then retrieved the whiskey bottle from the washstand.

She popped the cork and took several long pulls. After the last pull, she wiped her mouth again and set the bottle back down on the washstand.

She glanced at Flagg, sneered, adjusted her pistols on her hips, and moved to the door.

Flagg made a gurgling sound. The bed creaked. Saradee stopped with one hand on the doorknob, turned her head toward the bed. Flagg lay with his right cheek pressed to the mattress, eyes slitted. His ass looked like a raw roast.

"For god sakes," Flagg croaked. "Untie me."

"Untie you?" Saradee threw her head back, laughing. "Sure."

She squared her shoulders at the bed, drew both her Colts. With the left one, she drilled a bullet through Flagg's left wrist.

Flagg screamed. It was a long, ululating wail, like the shriek of a mountain lion.

With the right, Saradee drilled a bullet through his right ankle.

The scream rose again, louder, pricking the short hairs at the back of Saradee's neck.

She swung the left pistol up, fired, and a neat round hole appeared in the marshal's right wrist.

The scream was much thinner this time, but before its echo had died, she'd popped a slug through Flagg's left ankle.

The bed shook as Flagg flopped around like a fish on a landed stringer, howling.

Saradee scowled. "Such a racket, Marshal."

She twirled both smoking pistols before dropping them into their holsters, opening the door, and heading into the hall.

She moved down the stairs, boots chinging.

Below, the broken-nosed bartender stood behind the bar, staring up at her and arching one sandy brow. The old Mexican sat at the same table he'd been sitting at before, only five or six cards spread out before him. He held the deck in both hands and stared up at her, smiling crookedly.

"I do believe I ruined a perfectly good bed," Saradee said as she crossed the main room to the batwings. She stopped and turned toward Baskin, who'd swiveled his head toward her. "I'll leave you another hundred on the porch."

She turned, hesitated, and turned back to the room. "Hawk headed west?"

Glancing at her over his right shoulder, still grinning, Rojas nodded with a caballero's flourish.

Saradee pinched her hat brim and pushed through the doors. "Good day, gentlemen."

"Good day," said Rojas. He chuckled and turned back to his cards. "Be careful out there. The trails are not safe for pretty, defenseless senoritas."

21.

WITHOUT MERCY

GIDEON Hawk rose up from behind a boulder on the canyon's northern ridge and, teeth gritted, raised his Winchester to his right shoulder.

He planted a bead on the hat of Deputy Bill Houston riding at the head of the four-man pack clomping along the canyon floor. Hawk let the bead drop into the V-shaped notch on the rifle's receiver. Houston turned toward him slightly, opening his mouth to speak to Press Miller.

"This one's for Juliana," Hawk muttered, and pulled the trigger.

The rifle leapt and boomed, the report echoing.

Houston's head jerked toward his left shoulder. He dropped his reins, and his horse screamed, rearing. Without a sound from his own lips, Houston sagged back off the dun's left hip, bounced off a boulder, and piled up in a cholla patch, unmoving.

"Jesus Christ!" screamed Galen Allidore, losing his own adobe-trimmed, bullet-crowned hat as his white-socked black horse sun-fished sharply.

Hawk grinned tightly. At first, he'd been appalled by the notion of killing lawmen, but it was easier than he'd thought. He hoped Juliana was watching from heaven, as he'd hoped Linda and Jubal had watched him hang Three-Fingers Ned Meade.

He drilled another round into the ground beneath the shifting hooves of Allidore's black, then grinned as the horse reared, throwing the deputy off its back and into the rocks near Bill Houston.

Lowering the smoking Winchester, Hawk glanced right. Press Miller had dismounted. As his horse scrambled off up canyon, reins trailing, Miller dove behind a boulder and snaked his own Winchester over the top. Hawk jerked his head behind his cover as Miller's rifle popped and the slug slammed into the boulder in front of Hawk, spraying shards as the bullet ricocheted.

Hawk lifted his head above the boulder, extended his Winchester toward Miller, grunted a curse, and fired two quick rounds a half second after Miller ducked. Another rifle shot exploded to Hawk's left.

Hound-Dog Tuttle had dropped to one broad knee in the middle of the trail, his horse's dust still sifting around him as he jacked another round into his Winchester's breech and aimed the barrel up the ridge.

Hawk ducked, turned, and pressed his back to the boulder. Tuttle's slug blew up scree on his right.

They were making a game of it. That was all right. He needed all the practice he could get.

He pushed off his heels and ran straight up the ridge, another slug spanging off the rocks to his left. He dodged behind a witch's finger of sandstone, and another slug blasted the finger, spraying shards on both sides.

Hawk edged his rifle around the finger's left side. Below, the three surviving deputies were scrambling up the ridge, dodging behind cover.

His death's-head grin in place, Hawk levered and fired three times. When his smoke and dust were settling, all three deputies had gone to ground behind boulders. Gritting his teeth, rage and fury blending to turn his blood black, Hawk snapped off two more shots, then gave a whoop, dashed out from behind the finger, and scrambled straight up the ridge.

He glanced left and up, where Juliana's lifeless body lay concealed in the rocks. A fresh wave of rage washed through him, making his heart pound. Switching course slightly, skipping and leaping over stones and holding the Winchester in his right hand, he ran northeast toward the sharply pitched, sun-baked boulder field near the ridge's notched crest, a good three hundred feet away.

He'd lead these bastards toward the ridge, kill them one by one along the way, and let the buzzards and desert wolves scatter their bones along the rocks.

Two rifles blasted simultaneously, the slugs plowing sand and gravel a good ten feet below Hawk's heels. He stopped, turned, fired two quick shots toward Allidore, another toward Hound-Dog Tuttle farther down the ridge, then leapt behind a knob from which a spindly cedar grew.

A bullet punched into the cedar, which folded over itself with a crackling sound.

Press Miller's voice rose from several yards down the ridge. "Galen! Hound-Dog!"

Hawk doffed his hat and, crabbing forward, edged a look over the knob. He saw part of a hat thirty yards below and right, between two rocks. He recognized it as Miller's Texas-creased, black Stetson, with a braided leather band. The hat jerked to and fro, as though Miller was sending hand signals to the other two men spread out along the ridge to Hawk's left.

Seconds later, keeping their heads down so that Hawk could see only the tops of their crowns, the men spread out across the ridge, no doubt intending to surround him.

Hawk peered up the rocky, cactus-studded slope turning russet by the westward-falling sun, shadows angling out from the rock formations. A hundred yards up and right, two rock palisades rose from a vast crag of solid, black granite.

He scrambled out of the hollow and, swinging his gaze behind, catching glimpses of all three deputies spread out

and moving toward him, ran straight up the ridge. He zig-
zagged around barrel cacti and boulders as his pursuers
fired from below, most shots either too high or too low,
though one carved a notch from his right boot heel.

"Come on, you sons o' bitches!" he shouted. "You
wanted me. Here I am!"

Fifteen minutes after leaving the hollow, he gained the
granite crag. He ran a hand along the pitted and fissured
stone wall as he cast another glance behind.

He could see only Miller and Tuttle from this angle,
crouching and climbing toward him, slipping in scree and
dodging behind cover. Tuttle had lost his hat and, in the
cool, still air, Hawk could hear his labored, rattling
breaths. Hound-Dog was one of the best trackers Hawk
had known, but his overindulgence at the supper table
made him useless without his horse.

Hawk wheezed a laugh through his own labored
breaths, then moved farther up the slope and turned and
began climbing the crag, probing the eroded wall for hand-
and footholds. He used only his left hand, as the
Winchester occupied his right. He was two-thirds to the
top of the main scarp when a bullet barked into the wall
about six inches to his right, showering his face with granite slivers. Several stung like spider bites.

A wink later, the report echoed from behind.

As small streams of blood dribbled from the rock slivers in his cheeks and forehead, he cast a look over his right
shoulder. Fifty yards away, Press Miller crouched behind a
greasewood shrub, ejecting the spent shell from his rifle's
breech.

Hawk turned back to the wall and barreled up and over
the top as another slug slammed into the wall, the shot re-
verberating around the canyon, nearly drowning out
Miller's shouted epithet and the metallic rasp of his rifle's
cocking lever.

Hawk moved to the opposite side of the crag, his boots
crunching the fine, black gravel and dried bird shit, the
sandstone palisades rising on either side and a hundred feet

above. At the far side, he dropped to a knee behind one of
the towers, edged a look down slope.

Galen Allidore was moving up through boulders and
catclaw, crouched over the dusty rifle he held in both
hands, his gray duster flapping around his six-shooters and
black denims. Allidore was peering sharply to Hawk's
right, a quizzical frown pinching his features.

Hawk snugged the Winchester to his shoulder, aimed
down the barrel, waited for the deputy to clear two wagon-
sized rocks. "Turn back, Galen," he shouted. "Go back to
your kids. I don't want to kill you!"

Allidore whipped his head from left to right. Looking
up, he spotted Hawk and snapped the rifle to his shoulder.

Hawk pursed his lips and fired. The shaggy-headed
deputy screamed as the slug punched through his upper
right chest, blowing him off his feet. He landed on his butt,
back resting straight up and down against a boulder.

He dropped the rifle, which rolled off his thighs. As he
clutched the wound, grimacing, Hawk racked another
shell, aimed, and fired.

This round punched through the middle of Allidore's
chest, killing him instantly, his legs jerking as his torso slid
slowly groundward.

Before Allidore's hatless head hit the gravel, Hawk
turned and ran back to the other end of the scarp. Both
Miller and Tuttle were running toward the crag's base, hat
brims shading their faces. Miller was coming from farther
away, so Hawk crouched and shot Hound-Dog Tuttle's
right knee out from under him.

Hound-Dog dropped to both knees and screamed. To
his right, Miller switched course and ran toward Tuttle.

One hand to his bloody knee, Hound-Dog raised his
head, face etched with pain, bellowing like a poleaxed
mule.

"Crawl back behind the rocks!" Miller shouted at him.

When Miller was fifteen feet to Hound-Dog's right,
Hawk cocked and aimed, pulled the trigger. A neat round

hole blossomed in the middle of Hound-Dog's sun-bronzed forehead.

Hawk quickly ejected the spent shell and looked at Miller. The senior deputy had stopped in his tracks, shuttling his exasperated glance from Hound-Dog to Hawk.

Hawk planted a bead on Miller's badge winking in the fading light. As he squeezed the trigger, Miller dove to his right. He leapt to his feet and dove behind a boulder as Hawk again triggered the Winchester, the slug clipping the boulder's lip and spraying adobe-colored sand.

Hawk turned, edged around the northernmost palisade, and followed the scarp to where it feathered into the ridge, then resumed climbing. The terrain grew rocky and boulder-strewn, and he hopped from rock to rock.

Reaching the crest, he peered down the opposite side. A deep, brown barranca dropped away, a corduroy landscape much like the canyon Hawk had just climbed out of. There way no way into it from there, however, as the ridge was a sheer rock wall five hundred feet deep.

Hawk turned around. Miller was scampering up the rocks, dropping to his knees as he slipped in talus slides and tripped over cactus, aiming his Winchester uphill in his right hand.

Hawk leapt onto a boulder then dropped into the hollow on the other side, the sharp, geometrical lines of tumbled boulders surrounding him. There was no comfortable place to sit, so he leaned back and twisted his torso slightly sideways, his legs wedged among the slab-sided rocks. He rested his rifle on a rock edge and ducked his head, so he wouldn't be seen from down slope.

He waited, thumbing the Winchester's stock.

He craned his head to stare through a slight gap between two boulders above him. Beyond the gap, a shadow moved, and there was the slight ching of a spur, the rake of a boot heel.

Hawk set his right boot, straightened, and lifted his head above the hollow. Miller stood twelve feet away, on a titled rock slab, crouching and looking to Hawk's left.

"Right here, Press!" Hawk snaked the rifle over the boulder before him and tripped the trigger.

Miller dodged the bullet, swung his own Winchester toward Hawk. The rifle spoke, tearing up shards before Hawk's face. Hawk blinked as he cocked the Winchester, tracked Miller, and fired.

Miller sidestepped from the bullet's path as he cocked his own weapon and fired again.

Hawk ducked, lifted the Winchester, emptied it into the air over and around Miller's bobbing head. As Miller, who'd clambered into a shallow notch to Hawk's right, blasted away with his own rifle, Hawk dropped his Winchester and clawed his Russian and his Colt from their holsters.

If anyone had been in the area, they would have thought a small war was being played out atop that ridge. The two men fired without pause, most of their rounds hammering only rock, until Hawk's pistols clicked on empty cylinders.

He pulled his head back into the hollow, dropped the Colt into its holster, and, choking on his own wafting powder smoke, flipped open the Russian's loading gate. His ears rang from the din.

He'd gotten only three shells seated in their chambers before a shadow passed over him.

"Put it down, you son of a bitch!" Miller's taut voice was a decibel higher than the ringing in Hawk's ears.

Hawk's hands froze. He looked up. Miller stood over him, a black-gripped Colt Army extended in his right hand, the hammer cocked. Miller's lips shaped a diabolical smile, one eye squeezed nearly closed.

"Climb on out of there or die like a rat in its hole."

Hawk stared up at him, his face burning. How could he have let a tinhorn like Press Miller get the drop on him? He should have kept one gun loaded.

For a second, he considered flipping the Russian's loading gate closed, spinning the cylinder, and taking his chances with the three seated shells. But he'd no doubt be dead before the loading gate had fallen against the pistol's silver chasing.

"Drop 'em both," Miller growled.

Hawk cursed silently, squeezed the gun in his hands as he stared up at the deputy. He could put the Russian to his own head, deny Miller the satisfaction. But then, he'd never respected suicide. Miller's spruce-green duster danced about his scuffed, stovepipe boots.

"Drop 'em both," Miller repeated, edging his voice with menace.

Hawk shrugged, set both pistols at his feet, grabbed the boulder ledge above, and began climbing out of the crypt-like hollow. Miller stepped back, turning sideways and aiming his Colt straight out from his shoulder.

The deputy was partially silhouetted by the falling sun, but enough light reached his face to show the several bullet grazes and cuts from rock shards. Blood shone on the top of his right shoulder, where his duster was torn.

Hawk stood before him, raised his hands shoulder high. He offered a sinister smile. "Well, you got me, Deputy. I'm all yours."

"Put your hands down."

"Don't you want to cuff me?"

Miller steadied the pistol in his hand, aiming down the barrel at Hawk, one eye nearly closed, the other reflecting the sunset's copper-lemon glow. "Why would I wanna do that?"

Hawk hiked a shoulder, pulled his lips farther back from his big, square teeth, which glowed against his sun-blackened skin. "You're gonna take me in, aren't you? Isn't that what you *law-abiding* lawmen do?"

Miller's revolver shook slightly as he bunched his lips with fury. "You're gonna die right here, you murderin' bastard. Just like you killed my partners. Without mercy."

"That makes you just like me, then, doesn't it?"

When Miller said nothing, Hawk laughed, throwing his head back. Miller's dark face turned even darker as he stared down his pistol's barrel at Hawk, whose guffaws climbed to a crescendo and echoed around the ridge.

Behind Miller, crabbing along the rocks toward the ridge, another person appeared. Saradee Jones approached and stopped about twenty yards down the ridge, extending both pistols toward Miller.

Laughing, Hawk gave no indication he'd seen the girl, but kept his eyes riveted on Miller, watching Saradee in his vision's periphery.

Slowly, Saradee lowered her matched Colts, a strange, haunted look in her eyes as she slid her gaze to Hawk. He cast a casual, fleeting glance at her, and could tell by her expression that she wasn't going to shoot Miller.

She was waiting for Miller to shoot.

Hawk didn't blame her. She knew that, sooner or later, when the exhilaration of the cat-and-mouse game ended, and the thrill of their bizarre couplings diminished, it was going to come down to either him or her.

This way, she didn't have to kill him herself.

Hawk felt nothing. No emotion whatever save a hilarious irony and a vague relief that it was all over. He wished he'd been able to kill Miller for Juliana and the hypocritical law Miller represented. Shit, Flagg and this tinhorn would probably return to Denver heros.

But Hawk had known going in that taking them all down was a long shot.

Hawk laughed at the vast mirth of it all.

A muscle in Miller's cheek twitched. He squeezed the Colt's trigger. The hammer clicked against the firing pin.

Hawk's laughter ceased, the echoes continuing to chase themselves around the canyon as Miller stared, horrified, at the empty pistol in his hand. He thumbed back the hammer, pulled the trigger.

Click.

He tried again, gritting his teeth.

Click.

Hawk chuckled.

Finally, Miller tossed the revolver away and charged,

bellowing like an enraged bull buffalo and swinging his right fist back behind him. As he neared Hawk, he brought the fist forward, spittle spraying from his gritted teeth.

At the last second, Hawk bent forward. Miller's fist whistled over his head. Hawk shoved his right shoulder into the man's belly, wrapping his arms around Miller's waist. He straightened, pivoting back toward the ridge, flinging Miller over the lip, the deputy's boots kicking stones and brush.

"Noooo!"

Miller's shrill cry joined the screech of a golden eagle as the deputy sailed into the vast emptiness over the canyon. Falling, arms and legs spread wide, he stared at Hawk with terrified eyes, his mouth forming a dark, horrific circle. He grew smaller and smaller until, only a brown speck, his body was engulfed by the canyon's murky shadows.

Stitched deep in the growing evening breeze, Hawk heard the soft, crunching thud of Miller's body.

He stared into the yawning chasm for a moment, then slowly turned around.

Saradee stood where she'd been standing when she'd lowered her pistols. They were still in her hands. She stood with one hip cocked, regarding Hawk with a half sneer on her lips.

Hawk opened his hands. "Since you went to all the trouble of climbing up here, you might as well have shot him."

"Intended to," she said, her blond hair wisping about her face and toying with the brim of her man's hat pulled low. "But when I saw him with his gun on you, I thought, why not let him solve my problem for me? I'd have killed him right after."

Hawk spread his arms. "I'm unarmed. It's not too late."

"I'm tired of fogging your trail," she said, dropping her chin and pursing her lips. He thought he detected a slight sheen over her eyes. "I'm tired of trailing you around like a damn lovesick girl in pigtails, not knowing whether to fuck you or gut you with a pigsticker."

Hawk spat to one side and squinted at her. He'd gotten used to the idea of his death, and felt a vague disappointment that he was still here with his memories and his rage. "If you don't kill me now, eventually, I'll have to kill you. You're no better than any of the others I hunt."

Saradee smiled proudly, and raised her Colts. Aiming them both at Hawk's head, she thumbed the hammers back and slitted her eyes while her wide, rich lips formed a pantherlike smile. "That's a bonded fact, Gideon Hawk. Don't you forget it. Only problem is I'm prettier, and a hell of a lot better in bed."

She moved toward him, lowered the pistols, but kept them pointed at Hawk. She stabbed his belly with both barrels, leaned forward, and kissed him.

She sucked at his tongue, nibbled his lips. He didn't return the kiss, but, as she rubbed against him, groaning softly, keeping the Colts pressed to either side of his navel, he could not deny the animal pull of her.

His cheeks burned; his pulse throbbed. Part of him wanted to step forward and rip her blouse off her shoulders, exposing those magnificent breasts, then throw her down and set her to writhing beneath him once more.

Another part of him wanted to smash her with his fists, to blow her brains out with his .44s.

Chuckling knowingly, she kissed him once more, tenderly, then pulled away. She kept the guns snugged against his belly. "Until next time, lover."

She depressed the hammers, gave the guns a twirl, dropped them into their holsters, wheeled, and headed back down the ridge.

Hawk stared after her, until the southern canyon's shadows had swallowed her, and he was left alone with the wind and the gathering darkness.

Peter Brandvold was born and raised in North Dakota. Under his own name and under his pen name, Frank Leslie, he's written over forty action-packed westerns. Visit his website at www.peterbrandvold.com. Send him an e-mail at pgbrandvold@msn.com.

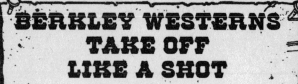

BERKLEY WESTERNS TAKE OFF LIKE A SHOT

LYLE BRANDT

PETER BRANDVOLD

JACK BALLAS

J. LEE BUTTS

JORY SHERMAN

ED GORMAN

MIKE JAMESON

Don't miss the best Westerns from Berkley.

penguin.com